DEADLY DARKNESS

VICTORIA ZAK

VICTORIA ZAK ROMANCE

Copyright

CONTENTS

Newsletter Signup Victoria Zak   v
Praise for Victoria Zak   vii

Chapter 1   1
Chapter 2   8
Chapter 3   16
Chapter 4   24
Chapter 5   30
Chapter 6   41
Chapter 7   50
Chapter 8   55
Chapter 9   63
Chapter 10   79
Chapter 11   87
Chapter 12   92
Chapter 13   101
Chapter 14   114
Chapter 15   122
Chapter 16   126
Chapter 17   132
Chapter 18   141
Chapter 19   147
Chapter 20   154
Epilogue   161
Book 3 Wicked Darkness - Sneak Peek   167

About Victoria Zak   175
More Books by Victoria Zak   177

Sign up for Victoria Zak's newsletter at her website to
receive a free ebook copy of her
Guardians of Scotland novella
Highland Destiny

You'll also find additional special offers, bonus content and
info on new releases.

www.victoriazakromance.com
victoria@victoriazakromance.com

1

TODAY WAS the day her life would end, Adaira felt it bone-deep as she ran through the glen like the devil was coming for her. For a fortnight, the dark fae prince had chased her in the woods, hunting her like prized game. He'd worn her down mentally and physically beyond exhaustion. She didn't know how much longer it would take before he stripped her of the will to live—to fight for what she believed in.

The prince played cat and mouse to perfection—leaving no doubt who the mouse was. One minute she'd be within his icy grip thinking she'd be returned to the queen, and the next, the prince would let her go—prolonging the inevitable for his own twisted amusement.

Hope of making it out of the glen alive was fading, but Adaira held on to the one thing that made her fight—her beloved sisters. They were depending on her.

The thought of her family gave her strength. She stopped and looked behind her. Although she was no longer being chased, it didn't mean she wasn't being followed. She dashed behind a tree, hoping to outwit the devil.

She leaned her head back and prayed the prince hadn't seen her. Her heart thundered as she anticipated another attack. Just the thought of returning to the Unseelie queen tattered her willpower. It was as if the queen was clawing at her, dragging her back inside a nightmare. A nightmare that Adaira had lived through for the past ten years.

Suddenly, something wet slid down her leg. Lifting her dress, she rubbed her calf. Blood soaked through her wool stockings and onto her hand. *Maiden, Mother, Crone?* She searched her body to find where the blood was coming from. A sting spread across her back and she reached over her shoulder, wincing as she swiped at her skin. Shite, the bastard had gotten her. It wouldn't be long until the fae poison entered her bloodstream where the bastard had slashed her back with his claws. She was doomed.

Adaira hung her head. That's when she noticed the bloodstained snow. The trail of blood led straight to her location. Nay! What was she going to do? The prince would surely find her now.

The earth suddenly shifted, causing her to freeze. No mere mortal would have felt it. The air around her flickered like a flame. The hair on the back of her neck stood on end from the powerful charge. He's here. There was no time to react; the prince swooped down from the sky and landed a few yards from the tree. Terror streaked down her spine.

He settled his great black wings and searched the area with his keen gaze. Adaira sucked in a breath, standing as still as the dead. The prince scooped up a handful of blood-soaked snow and inhaled deeply. Her essence was everywhere—the bastard would find her.

Adaira hugged the tree tighter, murmuring the only words of protection she could think of, Maiden, Mother, Crone. Spare me. Or just let me die before he finds me...

She gasped for air, finding the courage to fight. Surrendering wasn't an option. She needed to think clearly on how she was going to escape. Weak from blood loss, her muscles ached. Though she possessed unnatural strength, she wasn't immune to pain and suffering. And the wet cold had finally taken its toll. She needed rest and warmth— shelter from the prince.

The sound of snow crunching beneath his boots echoed around her. He was so close she could hear his heartbeat.

Oh, goddess, please. Please do no' let him see me. She closed her eyes and pressed herself flatter against the tree. The rough bark bit into her flesh like jagged teeth.

The prince crept past her like a fine mist floating through the glen. She cursed herself for being weak. If she had half her strength, she could attack him, rip his throat out, and personally deliver it to the queen. That wasn't going to happen. Instead, she had to outsmart the fae. She'd die before she'd allow him to bring her back to the queen.

Taking in a shallow breath, she eyed him again. He'd moved several feet ahead, studying the trees and ground in front of him. He knelt and scooped up another handful of snow. Adaira welcomed the distance between them, though it wasn't far enough.

Mayhap she'd live to see another night.

He stood and looked up into the sky. Slowly, he tilted his head from side to side like he was listening to something or mayhap someone. Fearing for her life, Adaira slowed her breathing as she kept her eyes pinned on the prince. He spread his massive black wings, stretching them wide. *What is he doing?* He knew she was here and weak. Why hadn't he gone in for the kill?

He crouched down, and with one pump of his wings, he flew up into the sky disappearing behind the clouds.

Dearest Maiden ... she sighed in relief as she peeled herself from the tree. She coughed through the coldness in her throat. On shaky, weak legs she took a step forward, then collapsed into the snow. Her body was shutting down. All she wanted was rest; however, if she surrendered to exhaustion she'd surely die. The prince didn't give up on his prey this easily. He'd return—she had to keep moving.

With all her might, she found the strength to stand. She brushed the snow off her dress and straightened her spine. "Leana, I will find ye."

The day turned colder and darker as the graying clouds engulfed the sky. She shook her head as she continued trudging through the snow. The fae poison was slowly dulling her wits. It would kill her if she didn't tend to her wounds quickly. She couldn't remember how many days she'd been on the run, but the growing pain drove her to find shelter.

Adaira stopped abruptly and squinted through the snow flurries. Smoke billowed up ahead. *Where there's smoke there must be fire, and where there's fire, there must be shelter.* Could she trust what she was seeing? Or was this fae poison trickery? At this point, she hadn't any choice. If she didn't get the poison out of her body, she'd die. And if she stayed outside in the cold much longer, she'd perish from exposure.

Adaira forced her exhausted body to keep going. Black and silver tents dotted the landscape. She heard men's voices in the distance. Aye, this was a campsite, but whose? Why were they camped in the middle of nowhere?

She crept to the closest tent, the fire more inviting than anything she'd ever seen. Keeping watch, she warmed her hands over the flames. Her body slowly tingled back to life as she prayed this wasn't a dream, that she wasn't lying in the snow somewhere dying.

But death visions didn't include the smell of smoke or fine ash drifting high in the nighttime air. This had to be real.

The frigid wind shook the tent, startling Adaira. She quickly retreated into the shadows, waiting to see if anyone would come out. She shivered, imagining herself inside the shelter, tucked beneath a thick fur with a bowl of hot broth in her hands. Her knees buckled. The poison smoldering in her veins was spreading. Someone had to be around to help her. Were these honorable men or beasts like the prince? Would they assist her?

Before she collapsed from exhaustion, Adaira staggered through the snow to the tent and walked in. "Hello?" The word came out as a mere whisper.

When no one answered, Adaira stepped deeper inside. She rubbed the cold from her arms as she looked around. A fur pallet was situated on one side and a sword and water skin were laid out next to it.

Another sharp wind rattled the canvas, but this time it was different. It howled with warning. Adaira's gaze zigzagged across the shelter as the shadow of a wolf appeared on the outside. Consumed with fear, she knew she didn't possess the strength to fight. She moved quickly, grabbing up the sword, ready to strike if she had to. But the beast was nowhere to be seen.

This wasn't over. It couldn't be. Wolves were as relentless as the dark prince. The bloody bastards hunted in packs and didn't give up—not until the hunt was over—until their prey was dead. Adaira wasn't ready to enter the barren realm of death— she'd fight. If they wanted her, they'd have to come and get her.

A wolf howled and three more shadows appeared, circling the tent. "Show yerself, wolf," she cried out with the last bit of strength she possessed, the sword almost too heavy to lift.

She followed the shadows around the inside of the tent, ready to pierce their furry flesh through the heavy material. Her back was facing the tent's entrance when a cold blast of air rushed inside. A wolf had entered the tent. She felt its breath on the back of her neck.

Heeding her instincts, Adaira whirled around, the sword raised high in the air. A gray wolf stalked closer, snarling and snapping at her. *Shite, the poison.* Would she even be able to swing the heavy weapon? Surely the beast could sense her weakened state and smell her fear. Any sudden movement would invoke an attack.

Too weak to hold on to the sword, it dropped from her hand. The beast lunged and she squeezed her eyes shut, ready to feel its sharp teeth bite into her skin. When she didn't end up on the ground with the wolf gnawing at her neck, she opened her eyes and gasped.

The world was spinning as she staggered forward, finding a naked man with long dark hair streaked with gray standing in front of her. She reached out and touched his face, burying her shaking fingers in his thick beard. Familiar silver eyes bore straight through her. By the saints, she knew those eyes, for they haunted her dreams.

"Rafe?" She swayed and fell forward. Strong arms caught her, pulling her into a wall of pure muscle and warmth.

"My heart's queen." The rugged voice she knew so well soothed her aching body. His words assured her safety. "I will take care of ye."

Adaira rested her head on his chest, letting him hold her up. "Rafe," she swallowed, struggling to talk. "Poison."

"Shhh, let me take care of everything."

Adaira's world faded into a black void, but her heart was safe.

2

WAS HE DREAMING? Was he holding the woman he loved in his arms? Rafe looked down at the lass. He brushed a strand of black hair from her face. Flawless pale skin...full red lips...high cheekbones. "Have my eyes deceived me?" He caressed her face ever so gently. "My queen." Rafe picked Adaira up, cradling her close to his chest. "What has happened to ye?"

He laid Adaira on the bed. Bewildered, he hovered over her. His heart skipped a beat as pale, blue eyes looked up at him.

"Rafe," she moaned. "Help me." Her eyes shut.

Thank the gods he'd called his men off before he entered the tent. One second later and she'd have been ripped limb-from-limb. He took a step back. Adaira, the woman he'd been ordered to hunt down and bring back to Cormag, was lying in his tent.

Rafe shoved his hands through his hair, then paused. He noticed a smear of black blood on his arm. Struck with worry, he gently rolled Adaira over. The back of her dress was shredded and blood oozed from slashes across her flesh. Rafe ran his finger through the blood, then sniffed it. "Fae filth," he growled.

Rage boiled through his veins. The fae who had dared hurt Adaira would pay.

"Milord."

The disruption made Rafe jerk. Quickly, he threw a fur over Adaira before anyone could notice her.

"Did ye catch the intruder?" Ranger asked.

"Aye, and the wench will pay for trespassing," he seethed and nodded to the lump of furs with a wicked grin.

Ranger's lips curled in approval. "A lass?"

"Aye."

"What business does a lass have here out in the snow?"

"I don't know, but I'll find out."

"Here." Ranger handed Rafe a tankard of mead. "Ye'll be needing this to quench your thirst. It might be a long night." He winked.

"Aye." Rafe gestured for him to get the hell out.

Ranger nodded and left.

Alone with Adaira again, he turned back to the pallet. She groaned, and Rafe knelt beside her. Having the woman he was expected to capture in his tent was dangerous. No one could know she was here. He threw the furs back and then ripped her dress open. Her condition was much worse than he thought. The wounds were deep and she had lost a lot of blood. Grabbing one of his tunics from the floor, he blotted the blood and cleansed the wounds with mead. He needed to get a better look at them so he could determine what to do.

Rafe had been playing with fire the day he set eyes on Adaira. She was the daughter of the laird who had given his pack protection. Once he looked into her blue eyes, there was no turning back. His wolf yearned to protect her, a sign he couldn't ignore. No matter how many times Adaira had pushed him away, there was no denying that she was his mate.

Doughall Keith was a complicated man, yet Rafe remained loyal because Doughall had given him a home—a new start in life. Rafe's kind wasn't welcome in Scotland, not after endless rumors had spread across the seas about the mad wolf who'd slaughtered hundreds of the Welsh. But the tale fell on deaf ears in Doughall's hall. The pack's savagery and abilities intrigued the laird, and was exactly what Clan Keith needed to defend their land from Clan Gunn. That's how the Honor Guard was created.

However, he never dreamed one day he'd be hunting the woman he loved. Under Cormag's rule, the Honor Guard turned into nothing more than the laird's attack dogs, taking care of his dirty work. When Adaira and her sisters were accused of murdering the laird's son, they fled Dornoch. Rafe was ordered to bring them to justice. There was no way in hell that he'd remain loyal to a man who vowed to destroy the one thing that was good in his life. Protecting Adaira overshadowed the risk of going against the laird's orders. He'd lost Adaira once, he wasn't losing her again. Not even his pack could stand in his way.

His pack was honorable, but with a hefty bounty on the Keith sisters' heads, greed clouded their judgment. No doubt, he played a dangerous game. If Cormag found out he aided the Keith sisters, he'd burn with them.

He finally stopped the bleeding, yet she still reeked of poison. He stood and walked over to his satchel where he pulled out a bag of dried mint leaves. Many times, he'd used such leaves to heal his own wounds. It would relieve some of the pain, too, but fae magic was tricky. Only the fae could reverse its effects.

Rafe sat down next to Adaira and gently covered the wounds with the dried leaves. Her flesh, cold and pure as fallen snow, beckoned him. It had been too damn long since he'd held her in his arms. He slid his hands down her ribs, gently caressing the sides of her full breasts. Aye, his dark angel had come back to him.

Mesmerized, he fell deeper into Adaira's spell. By the saints, he'd missed her. He hadn't seen her since the night she'd left Dornoch. A memory surfaced of that night. While everyone was celebrating Samhain, Adaira had met him at their secret place, behind the castle near the cliff's edge. Waves crashed against the rocky shoreline below. Adaira had been lying beneath him beautifully naked, her black hair fanned out over the grass. Her eyes twinkled like sapphires in the moonlight. He licked his lips, remembering her sweet, tender mouth and the taste of salt on her skin as he'd kissed her body. Her breathless moans of pleasure escaping her were like heaven to his ears. Aye, the smell of sex had been in the air. That night, a wild passion burned between them.

Rafe took in a shaky breath. Memories like these were what good dreams were made of. They were the dreams that chased away the darkness. They were the dreams that kept hope alive that one day Adaira would come back to him.

Frustrated, he fisted his hands and growled. "Adaira, do not go where I cannot follow."

She shivered in response, needing warmth. Quickly, he rolled her over and removed the rest of her wet, blood-soaked dress. He gathered the furs around her, then sat beside her and rubbed her body through the thick material. What he was doing wasn't enough. She needed more—she needed his body heat. He stood and undressed, anxious to slip under the covers and hold her close. Pulling back the furs, he got into bed and wrapped his arms around Adaira, holding her close to his chest. She nuzzled against his body. "That's it my queen, take all that ye want."

He brushed her hair away from her face and kissed her forehead, praying her body had enough strength to fight off the poison. Losing her would be the death of him. The thought of never seeing or touching her again ripped him up inside. He stifled a mournful howl and tightened his arms around her. "Mark my words, I will kill the fae who did this to ye."

He didn't know how long he'd been lying next to Adaira watching her sleep, but it was long enough for the fire outside to burn out, for the cold air had invaded his tent. Reluctantly, Rafe forced himself from beneath the furs, tucking the covers tight around Adaira. He needed to tend the fire before he fell asleep. "Shite." It was cold. His bare arse was freezing even for a wolf.

Rafe wrapped his plaid around his waist before he stepped outside. The frigid air hit him hard. It burned his lungs as he inhaled, making him want to shift. In wolf form the cold wouldn't bother him; it was his human side that suffered.

He dusted the snow from a pile of wood near the tent and suddenly sensed he wasn't alone. As he carried the logs to the fire pit, he noticed his younger brother walking over to him.

"Tegwyn, what are ye doing up this early?"

"I'm coming back from watch duty."

"Aye." Rafe continued tending to the fire, avoiding further conversation.

"Aren't ye going to ask me about the Keith lasses?"

This was the last discussion he wanted to have with his brother. Time was running out; his pack was sniffing around. They knew Rafe had been acting strange. They'd been so close to capturing Masie they didn't believe she had escaped on her own. With Masie safe at Ravens Landing and Adaira in his bed, there was only one sister unaccounted for. And once Leana was found, then what would he do? He knew damn well he wasn't going to hand them over to Cormag. However, if he refused, his brothers would pay the price and he couldn't allow the Honor Guard to be punished for his crimes. If he didn't tread softly, he'd find himself banished from the pack and his head on the chopping block. And with a past like his, there would be no consideration for a second chance.

Rafe blew out a frustrated breath. "Well, did ye catch one?"

Tegwyn stood next to Rafe warming his hands over the fire. "Nay, but I find it odd that we had one cornered and she mysteriously got away."

"What are ye insinuating, Brother, that I'd deliberately let her go?" He turned to Tegwyn, sternly eyeing him. "I don't appreciate the accusation."

"Nay, I'd never question yer integrity. I'm a bit frustrated."

"Aye, ye know how to relieve that problem, don't ye?" Rafe smirked, shoving his brother in jest.

Tegwyn grinned. "Aye, 'tis been too long since a warm, soft lass has graced my bed."

Rafe knew the long hunt had taken a toll on Tegwyn. This winter was extraordinarily bitter, leaving few options for food. The Honor Guard had been hunting the Keith sisters for over a month and the pack was desperate for a hot meal, warm bed, and the company of women. He felt their restlessness in the air, which wasn't good—a restless wolf always meant trouble.

Because of Rafe, his brother and sister carried a heavy burden. They were known as the siblings of the Mad Dog. Rafe's violent reputation haunted him like a lurking demon, at a distance, yet close enough to torment his soul. Hell, after a while, he'd stopped fighting the darkness and welcomed it, accepting his fate. He didn't deserve to be forgiven for his sins—not after what he had done to Gwenlyn.

The taste of rage still lingered on his tongue and the sound of his fangs ripping into flesh still echoed inside his head. His sleep was dominated by nightmares of him uncontrollably racing through his village, ripping and tearing through people who crossed his wrath.

No matter how fast or far he ran, his past was always just one step behind.

It wasn't the nameless faces that he'd killed that haunted him from the grave. Nay, it was knowing in a haze of fury he'd killed his mate. It felt so fresh in his mind, Gwenlyn gasping for life as he held her. Rafe had ruined his family, because he couldn't control his temper.

"Brother, there's something ailing yer mind." Tegwyn faced him. "Do not allow the ghost in."

Aye, his brother knew him too well. Even through the hardest of times Teg stood by him. He didn't deserve his brother's loyalty, yet Teg loved him unconditionally. That only hurt Rafe worse, knowing he kept secrets from his brother. Secrets that could end up being the death of them.

"Teg, ye worry too much. I'm well. The hunt is wearing me down just like everyone else."

Tegwyn raised a brow. "And this has nothing to do with Adaira?"

Rafe shifted from one foot to the other. "Adaira made her choice when she fled Dornoch and took a liking to the enemy. She's the one who has to answer for her crimes." He felt the weight of Teg's scrutiny. "Do not question me, Brother. Adaira is no concern of yers."

"It is when my life is on the line. Rafe, if ye know where she is, ye must turn her in."

"I'm through having this conversation with ye," Rafe growled. "Heed my words, Brother. Adaira makes her own decisions, and the guard must fulfill its' duty to the laird. Don't question me again."

Tegwyn looked away as Rafe glared at him. A sure sign his brother fully understood the consequences of speaking Adaira's name.

Rafe didn't mean to be so gruff. He clasped Teg's shoulder. "We're no good in our current state. I'm calling off the hunt for a couple of days so we can all rest. We'll camp here until then. In the meantime, take the pack to the village. Find a tavern and some lassies to keep ye warm."

A grin spread across Teg's lips. "Aren't ye coming?"

"Nay, someone needs to stay here. Promise ye'll keep the men in line. Ye're in charge."

"As ye wish." Teg nodded and then made his way back to the campsite.

Rafe looked up into the early morning sky in relief. His brother's senses were right. How long could he keep up such treachery before he was caught?

3

As if in a weightless dream Adaira rose from the pallet like mist rising from a loch. A warm ray of light shined down on her, calling her soul from the darkness, reminding her of a time long ago when she and her sisters were free-spirited and frolicked in the sun. Masie and Leana's youthful giggles echoed in the memory as soft mystical whispers called her home.

When the soft voices fell silent, Adaira opened her eyes and stared blankly at her own corpse still lying on the pallet. There was no fear, no screams of denial, and no regrets. She wasn't afraid to die. "Ashes-to-ashes, fade to black. A new life begins." Her dispirited epitaph marked an end to a life that was extinguished long before she'd taken her final breath.

An icy awareness tingled through her fingertips as she touched her lifeless body. The furs fell flat against the pallet and she gasped, stumbling backwards. Her hand trembled as she flung the furs away and stared down into a mound of ashes.

A brisk wind invaded the tent whipping her ashes into a

cloud of dust, spinning the scene around her into a barren forest. Dead trees lined the bank of a murky stream that snaked through the forest. Ravens squawked and circled above. The stench of rotting earth surrounded her. *A sure sign of death*, she thought.

A chill raced down her spine as she walked deeper into the woods, entering the realm of the dead, forever damned. When she reached the stream, a fiery halo appeared above the flowing waters. Raging flames flickered toward the heavens, hissing like a whispering siren, luring Adaira closer. She tipped her head back and stretched out her arms, bathing in the warmth and accepting her fate.

She didn't know how long she'd been there when she heard a voice. At first, she didn't pay attention, for nothing mattered except staying in the light. "Go away," she whispered.

"Adaira, help me."

Through her blissful haze, she recognized the voice and spun around. "Hello?" she called out as she stepped from beneath the light.

"Ye must go back."

"Leana? Is that ye?"

Her sister revealed herself, stepping out from behind a rowan tree.

Adaira ran toward her, but the faster she went, the more the forest came alive. Branches grabbed her, slicing her skin like sharp fingernails. "Leana, dinnae go. I'm coming!"

Adaira's feet suddenly sank in thick mud. "Nay!" The earth sucked her deeper inside. She struggled against the bubbling sludge, fighting her way to Leana. *Maiden, Mother, Crone*, she couldn't lose her sister again. She stretched her hand out to Leana, but she was still too far away. "Where are ye? I promise I'll find ye."

In a gasp, Adaira lunged forward in bed. Her throat felt like she'd drunk sand, rough and dry. Where was she? In between her labored breaths and coughing, she took in her surroundings and panicked. Nothing looked familiar and she couldn't remember how she ended up in a tent. A gust of cold air nipped at her skin. She looked down and found herself naked.

The tent flap opened and Adaira realized she wasn't alone anymore. Before she could cover up, the man froze in his tracks as if he'd seen a ghost. She blinked, trying to clear the fog. She needed to see his face clearly. Was he a threat? Did he strip her naked and put her to bed last night? Not knowing what to do, Adaira rolled off the pallet. "Stay away from me."

The man came closer.

"Heed my words. Stay away."

"Adaira, 'tis me, Rafe."

Rafe? Nay. She wiped her eyes. Why couldn't she see clearly? There was only one explanation; this wasn't real, she was hallucinating. Rafe couldn't be here, she was far away from home. "I dinnae believe ye."

Confused, she stepped back. If she could only remember what happened, how'd she gotten here. Aye, she'd been running through the woods, chased by the fae prince. "Nay."

"Adaira, ye need to lay down. The poison is still strong."

"Poison?" She felt the sting of the claw marks on her back.

"Aye. Do ye remember what happened?"

"I dinnae know what is real anymore. I can no' see clearly."

Rafe approached her. Carefully, he claimed her hand and held it over his heart. "I am real. Ye are inside my tent. Ye have been poisoned by the fae."

Adaira breathed a sigh of relief. "Rafe, 'tis really ye?" She took a step forward and the tent began to spin. Her knees buckled, but Rafe's strong arms saved her from hitting the ground.

"Aye, my queen, 'tis me."

"I...must...find Leana." Adaira fought to stay awake—the darkness beckoned to her again.

"All in due time. Ye need rest." Rafe picked Adaira up and walked back to the pallet.

"She's in danger." Adaira tugged the furs off despite Rafe's efforts to tuck her in. "I must go."

"Shhh, Leana's a strong lass. Wherever she is, we'll find her, but not tonight. Ye'll be of no use to her in yer current condition. Rest and fight off the poison."

Rafe was right. She stopped struggling. Leana was strong, but it was her instincts or lack thereof, that Adaira worried about. The oldest of the three sisters, Adaira was the responsible one, the voice of reason. She kept them safe, or at least had tried.

Adaira laid back. Leana couldn't make it on her own. She worried, with the queen out for blood, any one sister alone couldn't outrun her. What if she was too late? By the saints, what if the queen had already found Leana?

Leana, I will find ye.

As she drifted in and out of sleep, she remembered the day their fate had been changed forever. As children, they'd been desperate to help their mother escape their violent father. Ale brought out the monster in him. Seeking a way out of their miserable lives, they followed the fairy fire into the glen one night. Leana believed this was their chance to rid themselves of Doughall forever.

"Doughall must die." She could still hear the

desperation in wee Masie's voice. No child should harbor such anger.

The memory of Queen Galanthus Snowdrop's words sent a chill down Adaira's spine. "It's the rule of the Unseelie; in order to take a life, we must gain a life. One of ye must come with me and live in my kingdom and learn our ways."

Instead of being separated, Masie, Leana, and Adaira all pressed their bloodied fingers together with the queen's, sealing the oath.

"We're bound by blood," the queen said. "This oath can't be broken."

Even then, Adaira knew they were making a horrible mistake. She tried to warn Leana, but she wouldn't listen. The queen had only asked for one of them. However, Adaira couldn't let Leana carry that burden alone.

This was the first time she couldn't save her sisters from a horrible mistake. A mistake that had woken their true nature and their thirst for blood.

Another wave of nausea hit Adaira, filling her with dread as the effects of the poison took ahold of her mind, opening old wounds. She tried to shake the bad memories off, but she was defenseless.

She rolled over, curling into a ball. *Ye cannot run from yer demons, child,* the queen's voice sounded from somewhere in the distance.

"My heart's queen." Rafe's hot breath against her skin comforted her. "Hold on to me."

She rolled into his embrace, burying her head against his chest. His big arms wrapped around her, cocooning her in warmth. He grounded her, everything else was pain and lies brought on by the poison.

"Rafe, the poison...." Her voice trailed off as she faded into another deep dream.

This time she watched a scene unfold when she was but ten and three, cornered in the buttery by her father and another man much older than she was. "Ye'll wed this man and bear me a grandson," her father seethed. Doughall grabbed her by the front of her dress and raised his fist.

Adaira watched herself relive her father's drunken tantrum. Rage consumed her and she couldn't hold back anymore. Adaira ran toward Doughall and grabbed his arm, protecting herself from the blow. But she moved right through him as if she were a ghost. She turned around and watched his hand came down like a hammer, striking the lass in the face and knocking her to the ground.

In a panic, Adaira knelt in front of her younger self. "Run. Run away, lass," Adaria warned, for she knew what was going to happen next.

The lass looked up and Adaira froze at the sight of the agony behind her dark eyes. The cold truth struck Adaira in the chest. This was the moment that had scarred her forever.

The other man walked through Adaira and grabbed the lass by the shoulders, picking her up from the ground. "Ye should show yer father respect."

She spat in his face, which only brought harsh punishment.

Adaira's heart raced with terror. Tears streamed down her cheeks. She couldn't prevent the nightmare from happening. And she couldn't turn away. Her shield was down. Unprotected, Adaira's wounds reopened. *Maiden, Mother, Crone, make it stop!*

The lass was pushed to the ground. She screamed, slapping the man's hands away from under her dress. "Have no' ye learned yer lesson, wench?" He smacked her, splitting her bottom lip open. "Be a good lass and obey yer husband."

Adaira tasted the blood in her mouth...the stench of ale on his breath...the feeling of complete helplessness. It all twisted in her gut as she relived the night her innocence was stolen. Like a thief, the man took what he wanted and left her in a heap on the ground.

Shaking, Adaira sat back on her heels. "Fight lass, fight."

The man climbed off her and looked down at her as he straightened his trews. There was no compassion in his eyes, no remorse, not even a kind gesture to help her off the floor. "Until next time," he slurred and grinned.

The killer inside Adaira begged to rip the man's throat out and feed it to the dogs. Seeing herself sobbing on the ground, violated, was beyond devastation. She wanted to cradle the lass in her arms and reassure her she'd have her revenge, that she'd take justice into her own hands and make sure that he'd never be able to use his cock to harm another lass again.

Adaira walked toward Doughall as he watched his own flesh and blood sobbing on the floor. The grudge she'd carried in her heart all these years was because of him. He'd made her suffer, even from the grave. These horrid memories were only a small part of the damage he'd done. She breathed heavily, anger flowing through her. "How could ye?"

A cold wisp of air settled on her hand and the hairs on the back of her neck stood. The lass was holding her hand. Tear-filled, dark eyes peered up at her. "Tell him...Tell him he's an evil man, a disgrace. Tell him ye hate him for harming us. Tell him ye'll meet again one day in hell where ye'll finally have yer revenge."

Adaira considered the child for a moment. Her black

hair neatly draped over her shoulders was free of tangles and sweat. Her dress was clean. Any evidence of that heinous act was now gone. She reached down and touched the lass' hair. Her hand passed through the strands and the girl melted away, along with her childhood hopes and dreams. Doughall had stripped her of everything in life. He'd raised the demons inside her. Adaira fisted her hands. Aye, she'd made sure justice had been served.

Adaira glared at her father. "Ye're going to die."

Doughall's image faded along with the earthy smell of the buttery and was replaced with warmth and the fresh scent of mint.

"Rafe," she sighed.

"I'm here. I won't leave ye."

"Is this real? It feels real."

Rafe placed Adaira's hand over his heart. "Aye, 'tis real."

Relieved, she inhaled the serenity around her and exhaled the remnants of the nightmare.

4

RAFE HAD SEEN a lot of death in his time, but nothing compared to watching someone wither under the weight of fae magic. He held Adaira in his arms as she slept and lightly stroked her arm. A full day had passed since he witnessed the last wave of poison ripping through her body. As time went on, the better her chances of survival.

She would be the first to beat it. Rumors said no one could withstand the pain, let alone face the demons that plagued the mind of the unfortunate soul suffering from the poison. His heart's queen fought like a warrior.

Mesmerized by Adaira's beauty, he caressed her cheek. She sighed, and he stared at her red lips. He brushed his thumb ever so gently across her bottom lip. The bitterness of their last kiss still lingered on his tongue, reminding him of the day she left Dornoch without saying goodbye. He touched his forehead to hers. Her skin was cool. The fever was gone. He breathed in her intoxicating scent. It brought him back to a warm, spring day in the glen where the wildflowers bloomed. Aye, the smell of sunshine.

He closed his eyes and leaned in further to kiss her. He

brushed his lips against hers, then felt an uncomfortable squeeze against his ballocks.

"Kiss me again and I'll squeeze harder until they pop."

Rafe swallowed hard, then opened his eyes. Adaira's cold, dark glare rendered him speechless. She was awake.

"Rafe, why are we naked and in bed together?"

He removed her hand from between his legs. "Now, I can talk more freely." He cleared his throat. "I found ye in my tent two days ago. Ye were cold and had been poisoned by the fae. My body heat was the only way to keep ye warm."

"I've been here for two days?" Adaira sat up, tucking the fur around her chest.

"Aye."

"I've wasted too much time. I must leave." Adaira climbed over Rafe to get out of bed. She searched the tent for her clothes. "Where are my clothes?"

Rafe stood and donned his plaid. "Ye aren't going anywhere. My men out there have orders from Cormag to bring ye back to Dornoch for his son's murder."

Adaira turned and faced Rafe, folding her arms across her chest. "Aye, I should have known the laird would send his dogs after us. How much is my head worth?"

"'Tis not like that, Adaira."

"Then enlighten me."

"Ye'd be happy to know Masie is safe."

Adaira's eyes widened. "Of course she is. I left her at Ravens Landing."

"Nay, lass. My men had her and Commander Kerr surrounded in a cottage about three days' ride from here. Thankfully, I caught Masie first and brought her to safety. She's under Clan Gunn's protection now."

"Ye mean to inform me that the loyal commander of the Honor Guard didnae turn her over to Cormag?"

Taken aback by her angry sarcasm, Rafe tried to understand why she still didn't trust him. It was absurd for her to think he'd harm her sister. He'd risked his life and betrayed his pack to save Masie. "Nay. I'd hope ye'd think better of me. I wouldn't hurt Masie."

"What am I supposed to think, Rafe, when the Honor Guard is under Cormag's thumb?"

He clenched his jaw; 'twas a challenge to stay silent. Being the wolf he was, his tempter ran hot. "Ye have some nerve, woman. At least my pack is loyal which I can't say about ye, can I?"

"What do ye mean?"

"What were ye and yer sisters doing in Ravens Landings? They are our enemies."

Adaira slinked closer. "Ye're jealous, aren't ye?"

Rafe ignored her ridiculous accusation and walked past her to a trunk sitting in the corner of the tent. Adaira followed him. "Ye think I left Dornoch to bed Laird Gunn, bear him wee bairns, and live happily ever after? Ye're a fool of a wolf."

A fool? Aye, he was a fool for loving an uncontainable creature. Rafe spun around and grabbed Adaira's shoulders, glaring into her eyes. "I saved yer sister and now I've saved ye. But ye still question my loyalty. Who's the fool?"

Rafe left her speechless as he let go of her arms. He turned back to the trunk and pulled out a tunic and trews. "Here." He tossed the clothing to Adaira. "These should fit. Ye won't find yer dress. I burned it. I didn't want the remnants of fae filth in my tent."

Adaira raised a black brow. "Ye let me in."

"Nay, ye trespassed." He grabbed a wrought iron pot and strode out of the tent.

The damn woman knew exactly how to get under his

skin. He strode over to a pile of fresh fallen snow and filled the pot, then placed it on the fire.

Why did he keep torturing himself, believing Adaira would ever change her stubborn ways and accept him as a lover? How many times did she have to push him away before he got it through his thick skull that no matter what, Adaira wouldn't love him?

Mayhap, she was smart for keeping her distance. Mayhap, he should do the same. The only thing that mattered now was keeping Adaira's pretty head attached to her neck while they found the true murderer.

The tent flap rustled and Rafe turned toward the noise. The air in his lungs seized as he watched Adaira walk out of the tent. Her long, black hair was pulled back into a braid and hung over her shoulder. Even in an oversized tunic and trews, the lass looked beautiful.

"Adaira." He walked up to her and grabbed her arm. "Ye cannot be out here. Someone will see ye." He tugged her back inside the tent.

"Let go of me." She yanked her arm free.

"I can't allow ye to leave. If one of my men sees ye, they won't hesitate to take ye to Cormag."

"So be it." Adaira raised her hands, surrendering. "I'm turning meself in."

Was she mad?

"What are ye waiting for? Take me to Cormag. Either I turn meself in to one of yer men or ye can do it. Either way, I'm going back to Dornoch."

"Are ye daft, lass? Ye'll be hung. I will not be responsible for yer death, Adaira." He turned away, hiding the rage bubbling inside.

"Rafe." His name on her lips was spoken so softly. His

bicep flinched as he felt her cold hand wrap around it. "I must return home and clear me sister's name."

Rafe exhaled a frustrated breath. "Please tell me ye're not responsible for Beathen's death."

"Nay, I didnae murder the laird's son."

Rafe turned back around. Her dark stare pierced his heart. "What happened that night?"

"I wish I knew. All I know is what Masie told me. She said she saw Leana lying naked with two men in the blacksmith's shop. Both were dead with puncture wounds on their necks." Adaira began to pace. "I begged them no' to go to the festival, but Masie wanted to pray for Mum. Leana, well, ye know how she is."

"Aye, she has a wild streak."

"Rafe, I want to believe Leana had nothing to do with Beathen's death. But in order to find out what happened that night, I need to go back home and search the blacksmith's shop. I can no' run from Cormag and the fae queen any longer."

Her desperate plea tore at his heart. He understood her need to protect her sisters. Hell, he'd brave the fires of hell to keep his family safe. "Lass, I cannot allow it. If something happened to ye—"

"Please, I need time to clear our names."

"And what if ye can't? What if Leana committed the murders? Then what, Adaira?" Frustrated, he shoved his hand through his hair. "Ye and yer sisters will be found out. Cormag is already suspicious about yer true nature. This is madness."

"I didnae have a choice."

"Aye, ye do." He cupped her face. "Let me keep ye safe. Let me deal with Cormag."

"This is no' yer fight, nor is it yer choice. I'm the oldest, and it's me duty to protect Masie and Leana. Being the Alpha of yer pack, ye should understand me decision. I'm going back to Dornoch with or without ye." Adaira walked away, heading out of the tent. If Rafe wouldn't take her as prisoner, she'd turn herself in to his pack.

"There's no changing yer mind, is there?"

Adaira halted. She turned and shook her head.

"Ye are one stubborn lass. I cannot let ye do this alone."

Adaira smiled. "Have faith. I'll find the truth, then find Leana."

Aye, he didn't doubt her determination; it was himself he doubted. He'd failed once in protecting the one he loved. Reliving that pain would be the death of him. As long as he kept his mind on the mission and his cock locked away, Adaira might have a chance at keeping her head.

5

RAFE PUSHED Adaira to the ground in front of his pack. "The Keith wench has finally been caught."

Adaira glared up at the salivating dogs surrounding her and hissed. The hatred in their eyes burned straight through her. "Aye, I thought I smelled the stench of Cormag's dogs."

A tall man dressed in armor unsheathed his sword and approached her. He snatched her up by her hair and held his sword against her neck. "That would be Laird Cormag to ye, murderer."

"Ranger," Rafe warned. "Let her go. She's no good to us dead."

Adaira looked at Rafe. It hurt him seeing her being treated this way, but she couldn't risk his pack becoming suspicious about her capture. No one could ever find out that she'd been right under their noses for the past two days. She'd do whatever it took to protect Rafe's loyalty to his pack. He had taken a huge risk for her and she wouldn't let him down.

Rafe stood behind Adaira. His hot breath wisped over her ear. "This is yer last chance to run, lass."

She breathed in his comforting scent. "Not a chance, Wolf."

"Have it yer way." Rafe motioned for Ranger to join him. "Tie her up good."

With a cunning grin Ranger nodded.

"William," Rafe called out. "Bring the cage."

In front of her, one of Rafe's men, on horseback, halted his steed. Behind the horse a cart was attached carrying an iron cage. Adaira swallowed hard. *Iron.* For a brief moment she regretted her decision not to run. She was still weak from the fae poison; the iron would only weaken her more.

The cage door creaked open and Ranger pushed her inside and closed the door behind her. "This ought to hold ye."

"Pray it does, because if no', yer throat will be the first I rip out." She grinned at him.

He grabbed her arm through the bars and yanked her close. Her skin burned as her arm touched the iron bars. Shite, the one thing Baobhan sith's feared the most, iron. Long exposure to the deadly metal would kill a blood drinker. Or, for the queen, it was a way to keep Adaira in line. She'd felt her skin melt away too many times. She didn't need these wolves finding out her little secret.

The smell of stale mead lingered between them. "'Tis best ye keep yer mouth shut, blood drinker."

Adaira hissed, displaying her fangs. "I do no' scare easily, dog." Even though Ranger showed no fear, the way he swallowed told her he was a frightened, wee lad.

Rafe rode up next to them. "Ranger, is there a problem?"

"Nay, my lord."

"Then stand down."

"Aye." Ranger nodded to his Alpha and retreated into the pack.

Adaira didn't miss the glare he threw at Rafe as he strode off. That wolf was trouble, for her and possibly Rafe.

"Give yer word that there won't be any trouble, Adaira. I cannot afford to lose more men."

"Then control yer dogs."

"Brother." A woman wearing armor and holding a shield rode up to Rafe.

Adaira never knew he had a sister.

"Teg sent me to inform ye he'll be here shortly. Something about a scent he'd picked up from the north."

Adaira met Rafe's concerned gaze and knew they were thinking the same thing—Teg was hunting Leana.

"How long has he been gone?" Rafe asked.

"Most of the morn."

"Very well, we'll head north. I'm leaving the prisoner in yer hands."

"Aye."

The woman eyed Adaira with a familiar silvery glare. There was no denying her similarities to Rafe. They both had dark hair except hers was missing the gray streaks. She was tall and lean and looked ready for battle in her impressive armor.

Adaira noticed the intricate wolf head design on her shield. It was the same design on the warriors' breastplates and on the banners the lower ranked guardsmen carried. There was much pride in this pack. In a way they reminded Adaira of her sisters and mother. They, too, had been unwaveringly loyal to each other and proud of who they were.

She missed her sisters dearly, and knowing she couldn't

protect them hurt. But that would all change soon. Mayhap, they were on Leana's trail and were close to finding her.

The jarring of the cart in motion threw Adaira to the back of the cage. The cold, iron bars seared her flesh through her cloak and tunic. She was careful not to show pain, because the last thing she needed was the wolves to find out they could torture her with iron.

On the second day of travel north, the weather turned brutally cold. The snow had no intention of stopping any time soon. Relief washed over Adaira as a village came into view. She could only hope that Leana's scent had led them here and her sister was safe inside. But Adaira knew better than to hold on to false hope.

Rafe motioned for the pack to halt. He dismounted and approached Ranger. Adaira moved to her knees, trying to overhear what the men were saying, but the howling wind made it impossible. Rafe nodded at Ranger, then he walked toward a tavern.

With Rafe gone, who would call off his dogs if one of them tried to challenge her?

Adaira pulled her hood up for extra warmth and sat in the middle of the cage waiting for Rafe to return. She felt like a little bird surrounded by salivating dogs waiting to eat her. She smiled; their barks were much worse than their bites. No one was going to kill her. Besides, Cormag wanted that pleasure.

"Ye see, love," Ranger strolled next to the cage, the devil in his eyes. "He won't always be around to protect ye."

Adaira kept silent.

"Look at me, wench." Ranger shook the cage. "I know the Alpha fancies ye, but I'll be damned if we all burn because of a blood drinker."

"Step away from the prisoner." Rafe's sister walked up to Ranger with her hand on the hilt of her sheathed sword.

Ranger grumbled something indiscernible before he trudged away.

Rafe's sister opened the cage door. "Did he hurt ye?"

Adaira shook her head.

"Give me yer word ye won't try to run and I'll let ye out."

"In this weather? I would no' make it far before I froze."

"Give me yer word," she demanded.

"Aye, ye have me word."

The woman helped Adaira down. She stretched, appreciating the chance to stand. Two days in the cramped space had worn her down. She hadn't fed in quite some time. A *Baobhan sith* deprived of blood was dangerous. Hunger dominated her emotions, making it difficult not to eye the woman's vein pulsing in her neck. Adaira licked her lips, struggling to control her instincts.

"Rafe said that the barkeep would allow us to stay at the tavern until the weather cleared." Rafe's sister untied her hands.

"Thank ye." Adaira rubbed her wrists. Why was she being nice to her when everyone else hated her?

"Come." She nodded toward the tavern. "Warmth and ale awaits."

Adaira gladly followed.

"I'm Seren," she called over her shoulder.

"Adaira, the blood drinker yer kind hates."

"Don't take it personally. They even hate their own kind."

"What do ye mean?"

"'Tis part of a wolf's nature, something ye wouldn't understand."

By the look on Seren's face, Adaira decided not to press

the issue. Instead, she'd stick to her plan to get back to Dornoch.

They made their way inside where most of the pack had sat down to a warm meal and ale. She followed Seren through the throng. Adaira noticed how most of the men averted their gazes as they walked by looking for a place to sit. The tension was thick, unnerving Adaira. Why were they acting this way toward Seren? Adaira accepted the hatred Rafe's people felt for her; it was natural. However, Seren was kin, the Alpha's sister and a fellow warrior.

A spot cleared at one of the tables and Seren motioned for her to sit. A man seated nearby glared up from his bowl and snarled, sliding further down the bench.

Before Adaira could ask questions, a skinny lass with a stained apron approached the table with two bowls. She couldn't be more than five and ten, Adaira thought. The poor thing shouldn't be here, not with a room full of restless, drunk wolves.

The girl placed the bowls on the table. "There be more in the kitchen."

"Thank ye," Seren said as she ate a spoonful of stew.

"Lass." Adaira leaned forward and right before she was going to ask her name, Ranger crept up behind the girl and wrapped his arms around her, squeezing her breasts.

Adaira watched in horror as the lass struggled to get away. Ranger was too powerful for her to fight off. The swine was going to end up hurting that lass, Adaira knew it. She had to stop him.

About to show the wolf her fangs, Seren seemed to read her mind and stood, brandishing a dirk. "Let the lass go, Ranger. She's only a child." Seren shoved the blade against his neck.

Ranger hissed in anger but let the girl go.

"Ye are not to touch that child or any other woman in this tavern. Do I make myself clear?" Seren warned.

Ranger laughed at her. "The only thing keeping ye safe is yer brothers. Can't ye see, wench, no one wants a female warrior in the pack? If I had it my way, ye'd be bearing my bairns and tending to my house."

"I wonder how Rafe would feel about yer disgusting opinions? I believe ye'd be banished for such views."

"Go ahead," Ranger spat. "Run to yer brother like a good bitch. I'm more valuable to this pack than ye."

Adaira watched Seren's demeanor change. The blade drew blood from Ranger's worthless neck. Was Seren going to cut his throat?

Adaira slammed her fists on the table and jumped up from the bench, hoping to gain Seren's attention. "Do no' kill him. He's no' worth ruining yer life over."

Seren didn't move at first. Adaira understood too well what it felt like to be consumed by hatred and rage. "Please, Seren."

Finally, she lowered the blade, looking defeated.

Ranger smirked as he walked away.

Without a word, Seren sat down and went back to eating her stew.

Adaira reclaimed her seat, too. "Trust me, ye did the right thing."

"Why did ye interfere?" Seren looked up from the bowl. "Why would ye care if I had killed him?"

"I know yer pain, lass. I've lived it. 'Tis a road ye dinnae want to travel. I'm no' blind. I see the way yer pack looks at ye."

"They despise me."

"Nay, they feel threatened. Do no' mistake their insecurities as hate."

Seren leaned closer. "I can best any one of them and they know it. My brothers have taught me well. I want to serve my people, but not by their standards."

"What do ye mean?"

"Women aren't allowed in battle. A good she-wolf is supposed to honor their mate and tend to wifely duties."

"And ye dinnae want that?"

"Nay." Seren's brows creased. "My heart is on the battlefield."

"Ye're brave to stand up to yer pack. However, I dinnae want to see their ignorance make ye do something daft like kill a guardsman." Adaira smiled. "We lasses must stick together. I like ye."

"And I, ye." Seren stared at her for a long moment. "Ye know, Rafe needs a lass like ye in his life."

Adaira coughed, choking on a sip of ale.

"Pardon me. I tend to speak before I think sometimes."

Adaira cleared her throat. "Yer words surprised me."

"I want to see Rafe happy. He's had a rough life."

"What do ye mean?" Adaira had known Rafe since she was ten summers old, before she'd made a blood oath to the fae queen. To think of it, she couldn't recall him ever telling her about his past.

"Ye haven't heard the rumors?"

Adaira sat back. Aye, she'd heard the rumors just like she heard the gossip about herself. Tall tales were just that —lies most of the time. Rafe didn't match the monster in their stories.

"Ye cannot tell him what I'm about to say."

Adaira nodded.

"Before our pack came to Scotland, our home was in Wales. Rafe was mated to a beautiful woman he loved dearly, Gwen. Life was good for us, until King Edward declared the extermination of all wolves."

"Why?"

"I don't know. 'Tis my guess he found out about our kind and wanted us all dead. When the king's campaign reached our village, it was best for us to welcome the hunters into our homes so the king wouldn't grow suspicious. Rafe and my father hated the fact we had no choice but to give them a place to sleep and food to eat. The king offered ten shillings a pelt."

Adaira couldn't believe what she was hearing. "I'm so sorry."

"My father and Rafe had enough. I'll never forget our last summer in Wales. Rafe prepared us for battle. When the hunters returned, we welcomed them with a surprise attack. The whole pack shifted. Unfortunately, pregnant women were easier targets, the hunters knew this. Before Rafe could save Gwen, he watched an Englishman plunge his sword into his wife's gut. She and his unborn bairn died in his arms."

Adaira gasped. "Och, Seren."

"Something dark changed Rafe that day. He slaughtered every hunter and sent their skins back to the king. Our people fled Wales to Scotland shortly after."

"Aye, I remember when Doughall welcomed yer pack into the clan."

"Let's hope the Mad Dog is never awakened again." Seren picked up her spoon and dipped it into the stew.

Adaira thought about what she'd heard. Her heart ached for Rafe. He'd lost a wife and his only child. He'd risked everything to protect his pack, and now, he was doing the same for her. If Cormag found out Rafe was disloyal to the clan, he'd burn. His family would be destroyed.

As the realization sunk in, she knew she couldn't allow him to keep protecting her. She would bring him more pain and suffering.

"Seren." A deep, rich voice Adaira knew well gained her attention. She looked up to see Rafe.

"Brother." Seren made room for him to join them. "Come, sit."

Rafe's gaze settled on Adaira as he sat down next to his sister. Adaira saw him in a different light now. She could see the suffering etched on his face.

"Any word on Teg?" Seren asked.

"Nay, no one has seen him, which is odd since his scent led us here."

Adaira was disappointed. She'd hoped there was news about Leana.

"The barkeep said the upstairs rooms are prepared," Rafe said. "Ye and our prisoner will sleep there. The rest of us will sleep down here."

"Brother, I can stay with the pack."

"Nay. They are restless and drunk. This is no place for a lady. Besides, I need ye to guard the prisoner."

Seren stood, obviously unhappy with her brother's orders. "I'm not daft. I can see she's not a prisoner. This is yer way of keeping me safe."

"Seren," Rafe warned.

"When will ye have faith in me? I'm a warrior. 'Tis in my blood." Seren strode off before Rafe could get another word in.

"Let her go," Adaira said as she touched his arm. "She's a smart lass."

"Aye, too smart for her own good," Rafe grumbled.

"Ye should be proud of her."

Rafe eyed her as he chewed his food. "Well, I see the two of ye have become close."

"Aye, I've grown fond of her company. Why dinnae ye tell me ye had a sister?"

"There are a lot of things I haven't told ye." He drank deeply from his tankard of ale.

Adaira watched his full lips press against the cup as he drank. The amber liquid washed down his throat and her gaze fixated on the long, thick vein running along the side of his neck. Her nipples strained against her dress as she remembered his touch. She knew the sweet torture those lips could bring. Being this close to him, smelling his spicy scent, awoke her senses. He always had this effect on her. The wolf mesmerized her beyond compare. She licked her lips.

A growl came from across the table. "Ye should tread carefully. My men are watching us."

Adaira shifted in her chair, extinguishing her lust. What was she thinking? She looked around the tavern—all eyes on her. Aye, she must not forget her place as a prisoner. "'Tis been a long two days. I'm going to bed."

Adaira started to rise, but Rafe grabbed her arm. "Sweet dreams, my queen."

His smoldering, silver gaze set her body on fire.

Adaira sucked in a breath. "I bid ye a good night, Wolf." She headed for the stairs.

6

Seren returned to the tavern after tending to her horse. Because she was the only woman in the Honor Guard, confrontations with Ranger and her brother weren't unusual. It was times like this when she doubted herself. She questioned her abilities as a warrior and wondered if she should give up just so there would be peace in the pack. Even though she knew Ranger was an arse, his insults still cut deep. She must prove the pack wrong. Skilled with the sword, she could best any one of these men, and they knew it.

The thrill of battle and the sense of pride that came along with it was what she lived for. But the distinction between honor and proving her worth became one and the same. Was she being stubborn? Mayhap, but she was born a warrior.

Seren remembered how her mother would scold her father for teaching their daughter how to wield a blade. She was the youngest of three and the only girl. She and her mother had different opinions about what she should do with her life.

"No respectable wolf would want a battle maiden as a mate." Her mother's words were as fresh in Seren's mind as the day she'd said them.

However, her father wanted his children to be happy. If fighting like a man made his daughter happy, he would make sure she was trained properly.

Now her happiness was creating tension within the pack, and between Rafe and her. Was it worth all the heartache just to prove a point? Was her thirst for battle that unquenchable that she was willing to cause a disturbance in the social structure of her people? If she was honest with herself, no.

She hated their scrutinizing glares and the way her brothers treated her with delicate hands. Why should she be treated any differently?

Seren breathed in the cold night air before entering the tavern. It was late, and most of the men were asleep. She crept through the throng of snoring men to the stairs and up to her bedchamber. Before she turned in for the night, she stopped to check on Adaira. She pushed the door open enough to peek inside. Adaira was asleep, so she shut the door. Confident their prisoner wasn't going anywhere, Seren entered her bedchamber across the corridor to freshen up before taking her post outside Adaira's chamber.

She splashed water over her face from the bowl on the table, and when she looked up, realized she wasn't alone. "Ranger, what the devil? Why are ye in my bedchamber?"

"This is where I belong, with my mate." Ranger's intense stare unsettled her.

Her instincts cautioned her to tread softly.

"Ranger, even though we are mates. I will not lay with ye. Now, please leave." Seren walked past him as she made her way to the door to see him out.

Ranger grabbed her arm. "I'm not going anywhere." His grip tightened and the smell of ale drifted between them. He was drunk. "'Tis time ye stop all this battle maiden nonsense and mate with me properly. A wolf cannot be denied their mate."

"I'm not ready to be mated. Until ye stop overdrinking, I will never take ye as my mate."

His grip tightened. "I do not have a drinking problem. Can't ye see what ye're doing to me by denying my right to take ye as my mate?"

Seren struggled to free herself. "Stop it," she winced. "Ye're hurting me."

"Seren," he said tenderly as he removed his hand from her arm. "I think about ye all time. Ye're the first thing I think of when I wake."

"Please, I beg ye not to do this. We can work this out."

"Nay, not when yer heart is on the battlefield. Ye'll never submit to me willingly."

The look on his face made her heart ache. Aye, denying him came with grave consequences. She'd resisted her wolf's call and was suffering, too. Ranger was right.

"I'm sorry. I'm not ready to be mated."

Before she knew what was happening, Ranger threw her over his shoulder and headed for the bed. Kicking and beating her fists on his back, she fought to get away. His large hand came down across her arse. "Ye'd be wise not to fight it, Seren," he warned. "Once I've claimed ye, yer role will be my wife, not the role of a battle maiden."

He tossed her on the bed and stood glaring down at her as he unbuckled his belt and then dropped it on the floor. Seren frantically moved away from him. "Ranger, ye're making a horrible mistake."

He grabbed her legs and pulled her beneath him. "The

only mistake I've made is not doing this sooner." He removed his surcoat, then his chainmail. "I won't allow yer stubbornness to tarnish my reputation as man and wolf. Ye will submit to me."

The bed creaked as he straddled her. Seren's heart raced when he leaned over, placing a sloppy kiss on her lips. She turned her head away. The smell of ale on his breath made her gut lurch. She pushed on his chest. "Please, Ranger, stop. Ye're drunk."

He sat up, looking down at her. For a moment, Seren thought he'd change his mind and leave. But knowing Ranger, he wasn't going without a fight. "Ye have left me no choice." He ripped the front of her tunic open, exposing her breasts. Seren desperately grabbed at the torn material, covering herself, but Ranger wouldn't allow it. He pinned her arms above her head with one hand while he squeezed her breast with the other.

Anger uncoiled inside her. No matter what he put her through, she wasn't going to give in easily. He shoved his hand down her trousers, grabbing her womanhood.

"Enough," Seren screamed and kneed him in ballocks. He rolled off her, and she bolted from the bed, heading to the door. As Seren reached for the latch, her head was yanked back.

Ranger had ahold of her braid and pulled her into his body. "Have it yer way, wench."

He pushed her hard against the wall. She cried out as her head slammed into the stone. "No, please," she pleaded as her vision blurred.

Adaira awoke with urgency. Someone was in trouble. Their

fear pulsed through her like thunder. She closed her eyes, honing in on their emotions. "Seren."

She leapt out of bed, grabbed her cloak, and left the room. Seren wasn't posted outside her door as she expected. In fact, there were no signs that she'd been there at all. Suddenly, raw terror throbbed in her chest.

A scream sounded from across the corridor. Without hesitation, Adaira shouldered the door open, splintering the damn thing to bits. Startled from the sudden disturbance, Ranger turned and snarled at her.

"What are ye doing here?" Adaira paused as she saw Seren's sword propped against the wall. "Where's Seren?"

Ranger turned around, smirking as he pulled up his trousers. "She's all yers." He stepped aside. To Adaira's horror, she spotted Seren pinned to the wall, her tunic ripped to shreds, her face as cold and emotionless as a corpse.

"By the saints, Seren." Adaira rushed over and covered her with a fur from the bed. "What happened? Did that bastard hurt ye?"

Seren kept her gaze on Ranger.

"He hurt ye." Seren didn't need to answer, Adaira knew by the lass' shaking body what that monster had done.

"I didn't hurt her," Ranger exclaimed. "I merely taught her a lesson."

She slowly turned around. Her vision narrowed on him. "Ye taught her a lesson?" Adaira approached the drunken fool.

"That's what I said." He stood tall with his hands on his hips, challenging her. "Punishments are not meant to be pleasant."

Adaira bit back the urge to rip his throat out. She wanted to see him beg for mercy before she slowly went in for the kill. "Nay, Ranger, punishments are no' meant to be pleasant, are they?"

He showed no fear, yet she could smell it rolling off him.

"But I must ask, what kind of punishment would a pack member receive if he was caught raping a woman who happened to be the Alpha's sister?"

"I—I didn't rape her." The tone of his voice sounded as if he was offended by her accusation. "She's my mate. A lesson needed to be taught. She'll be well by morn and back home where she belongs. Seren, tell her I'm right."

Adaira looked over her shoulder at Seren and her heart shattered. "Look at her, Ranger. Take a long, good look. Does she look well?"

Ranger glanced at Seren. Adaira saw a small hint of regret spread across his face. "'Tis wolf law. Ye wouldn't understand it."

"Ye're right, I dinnae. I will never understand a man taking something so precious from a woman or invading her body for his own selfish needs."

"What happens between my mate and me is none of yer concern. Hold yer tongue."

In a flash, Adaira slammed him against the wall, her hand at his throat. The large vein that ran down his neck throbbed against her grip. Even though Ranger was three times her size, she had the advantage. She could snap his neck.

Terror spread across his face as he fought to breathe. "I cannot...breathe." He clawed at her arms.

"Shhh, laddie. Ye said punishment was no' pleasurable." Adaira smiled with the devil in her eyes. She had no intention of killing him, only giving him a good scare.

"Ye wenches are all the same," he spat. "Ye need to be taught respect."

His warning infuriated her. A red haze blurred her vision. Ranger's face transformed into the monster that haunted her dreams. The monster had a face she'd never forget, the face of the man who had raped her.

The innocent lass she used to be surfaced. "Slay the monster," she whispered.

The lust for blood coursed through her veins. Long, sharp fingernails extended from her fingers as she gripped his neck tighter, lifting him off the floor. He kicked and gasped while Adaira stared at him, emotionless, watching the life force drain from his body. "Ye'll never hurt another lass again."

"Adaira." Rafe's voice thundered behind her. "Release him."

Adaira considered it for a moment. But anger mixed with vengeance was a deadly concoction. Even if she wanted to let go, the blood drinker inside her insisted on being fed.

"I said, release him." Rafe grabbed her arm, and she let go. Ranger fell to the floor holding his neck and sucking in air as fast as he could.

"Fucking blood drinker," he coughed.

Rafe spun Adaira around. "What is the meaning of all this?"

"This swine raped yer sister." Adaira looked at Seren.

"Seren, it this true?" Rafe asked. As he approached her, Adaira noticed how the lass avoided eye contact with Rafe. "Seren, tell me."

Before Rafe reached her, Seren shifted into a white wolf. She howled mournfully and then bolted from the room.

"Seren," Rafe went after her. "Come back." He stopped outside the door and spun around, anger evident in his eyes.

Good, Adaira thought. Rafe needed to be angry so he could punish Ranger.

Rafe strode back into the room and picked Ranger up by the back of his tunic, placing him on his feet. "Are ye well?"

Wait...what? Did she hear him right? *Are ye well?* "Are ye daft?" Adaira joined Rafe. "He raped yer sister and ye're asking him if he's well?"

"Adaira, stay out of this," Rafe warned.

"I will no'. This monster needs to be punished for his crime."

"Adaira," Rafe growled. "Ranger is Seren's mate."

"I dinnae care if this man is a saint, he has no right to touch her like he did."

Ranger finally came to. He glared at Adaira. "I told ye this was none of yer business." He held his neck as he walked past her and out the door.

Stunned, Adaira turned to Rafe. "Are ye going to let him go? No questions asked?"

Rafe shoved his hands through his hair. "Shite."

"Och, Wolf, ye better give me a damn good reason no' to go after him meself and rip his throat out."

"I cannot."

Adaira took a step back. "Why no'? She's yer sister."

"And a wolf. Under wolf decree, another wolf cannot interfere with matters of a mated pair. Seren has been denying her mate, which isn't good."

Adaira couldn't believe what she was hearing. "So, 'tis well for him to rape her into submission?"

Rafe sat down on the bed, resting his arms on his thighs. "I cannot get involved," he said.

"This is madness."

Rafe leapt from the bed and grabbed Adaira's arms, pulling her close. For a moment, her body betrayed her and she lost herself in his eyes. His glare heated her skin, making her forget how furious he made her.

"What do ye want me to do, Adaira? Kill him? That's murder. I'd be banished from the pack. A lone wolf is a dead one."

Adaira shook free from Rafe's spell. "I thought I'd never witness the day Rafe Madok would turn away from family. Seren needs you more than ever."

"And ye're crossing the line, Adaira. Wolves are different from *Baobhan siths*. We have a hierarchy, rules to follow. We cannot kill recklessly."

"Aye, thank the gods we are different. Yer wolf law is cowardly." Adaira spun around and rushed out the door. "I'm going after Seren."

"Adaira—"

"Nay!" She spun around, pinning him with a glare. "I will no' stand by and allow this to happen. Seren needs her brother, and if ye'll no' go after her, I will."

7

FURIOUS, Adaira rushed downstairs. On her way to the door, she strode past some of the Honor Guard, slumped over the tables and passed out from too much ale. To her relief, most of the men had retired for the night. As she reached the entrance to the tavern, a man staggered her way. "Where ye think ye're going, Keith wench? Ye're not trying to escape, are ye?"

Adaira abruptly halted. The sound of his voice made bile rise in her throat. She was in no mood to deal with another wolf.

"I asked ye a question," the man slurred.

Adaira charged him, grabbing by the tunic. "I will no' answer ye or any other man." She flashed her fangs.

His eyes were wide with fear as if the devil was staring back at him. "Please...I have a wife and children."

Adaira drew him in closer. "Then let me pass."

"Adaira," Rafe called from the top of the stairs. "Let him go."

She pushed the bastard away and he stumbled, falling to

the ground. She glared up at Rafe, hoping he'd had a change of heart about Seren. When he didn't make a move, she shook her head, disappointed. Letting Ranger go free after raping his sister was unforgivable. Wasn't Seren more important than some ridiculous wolf law?

Before she did something stupid, Adaira headed out the door.

It wasn't long before she found Seren's wolf tracks in the snow. Quickly, Adaira followed them behind the tavern. "Seren," she called out. "This is no' yer fault." The tracks led her into the woods where they disappeared. "Seren!" Adaira looked around, but Seren could be hiding anywhere.

A clump of trees moved up ahead. Adaira carefully approached. "Please, Seren, come out. I beg ye." Through the snow-covered branches, Adaira saw a set of vibrant blue eyes looking at her. She crouched and held out her hand. "Let me help ye. I know yer pain. Ye dinnae have to be alone."

Seren crept out from the bushes. Though in wolf form, Seren's shame was complete. Just the way she held her head with her shoulders sagging, demonstrated it. "Ye can trust me."

When Seren came within inches of Adaira, Rafe came running toward them. "Seren!"

The she-wolf snarled, then ran deeper into the woods.

Damn her bad luck. Adaira had been so close to gaining Seren's trust. Now she'd never be able to find her. She stood and faced Rafe. "Ye have poor timing, Wolf."

"Ye need to let this go."

"Let it go?"

"Aye. What happened between Seren and Ranger is their business. Tis wolf—"

"Wolf law, I know," Adaira said abrasively. "Mayhap if ye explain it I'll understand it better."

Rafe rubbed the back of his neck. "We do no' love freely, Adaira. Our mates are chosen for us when we're born. Wolves can't change that. Once a male has met his mate she's the only woman in his life that matters. 'Tis like they're woven into the very fiber of our being."

"Then why would Ranger hurt Seren if he loves her?"

"This is where it gets complicated. 'Tis not enough to be mates. To a male wolf he must claim his mate in order for them to be fully mated. He must...ye know..."

"Know what?"

"Consummate the union."

Adaira's eyes grew wide.

Rafe closed the distance between them and cupped her face. "Do ye understand why I cannot get involved?"

Adaira stood speechless as she absorbed this newfound information. Was she Rafe's mate? They had laid together. Was that his way of claiming her? Is this why he never gave up on her? She stared into his eyes. "Rafe, are we..." she swallowed hard, "mates?"

Rafe cleared his throat which was enough of an answer. Nay, Adaira couldn't, wouldn't accept this—she was not his mate. "Obviously, I'm daft." She stepped out of his embrace. "I dinnae know what I was thinking. I'm no' a wolf yer laws dinnae pertain to me. What yer laws lack in common sense, hurts yer sister. She's hurting right now and needs our support. How could ye allow that swine to walk away like nothing happened?"

"'Tis not my place."

"Not yer place? Ye are Alpha. Seren is yer family. What pricks my arse, ye didnae defend her."

Rafe crossed his arms, and Adaira could hear him

grinding his teeth, resisting the urge to lash out with hurtful words.

"Yer sister does no' deserve to be treated like she's beneath the men in yer pack. She's a warrior and deserves respect."

"Do not question my love for Seren."

"Then why didnae ye help her? She should no' be alone." As she recalled her own pain and suffering as a child, tears wet her eyes, but she held them back. "I know her pain, Rafe."

Rafe closed the distance between them. "There's much more here than Seren's situation, isn't it?"

Adaira averted her gaze. The walls surrounding her heart began to crumble. What she'd worked so hard to hide —her dark past and uncontrollable emotions connected to it—started to resurface.

"Adaira." Rafe tipped her chin up. "Ye can tell me anything."

Aye, she wanted to, but it wasn't that easy. Telling him would strip her bare, revealing a vulnerable side. As long as she had strength left in her body, she'd never reveal her weaknesses to anyone, not even Rafe.

Rafe cupped her face. "Let me in, Adaira. Nothing will ever change the way I feel about ye."

Adaira looked deeply into his sliver depths. "Once ye understand that I can no' return yer love the better off ye'll be." She pulled free from his embrace.

"Once again, Adaira Keith hides behind the same pathetic excuse that she cannot love." Frustrated, Rafe threw his arms in the air.

Adaira slapped him. "How dare ye."

Rafe turned his head slowly and glared at her. She'd never hit him before. Her emotions were out of control.

"Go on, push me away like ye always do." He grabbed her arm, pulling her against his chest. "Heed my words, lass. One day ye'll push me too far." He released her, then strode off.

Adaira stood speechless. Did she truly want the wolf out of her life for good?

8

ADAIRA MARCHED to her bedchamber and slammed the door.

"Wolf law," she spat. She would never understand it. Family was the only thing Adaira had left. She couldn't imagine walking away from them.

Seren didn't deserve this kind of treatment just because she was a warrior. Adaira prayed wherever Seren was hiding that she was safe. When and if she returned, Adaira could only imagine the consequences she'd face. And seeing how Ranger and Rafe showed no mercy when it came to wolf law, it wouldn't surprise her if Seren never came back. Mayhap, she saw too much of herself in Seren. Rafe was right about one thing—this was none of her business. And why should she care? The Honor Guard meant nothing to her. She owed them nothing, except for Rafe. It pained her to know he didn't want her help with Seren. All she wanted to do was save his sister from making the same mistakes she'd made.

Adaira blew out a frustrated breath and walked to the window. She pulled the fur covering back and a blast of cold air hit her face. She leaned against the stone wall and closed her eyes, welcoming the calming breeze. The wolf had a way of crawling inside her heart when she least expected it. She'd been so angry at him; however, she never meant to hurt him.

Over the past few days, he'd brought out old feelings Adaira had long ago buried. There was once a time she'd dreamt about having a future with the honorable wolf, but that was before her innocence had been stolen. Before she returned home a blood drinker.

He never judged her for being who she was. In fact, he was too damned understanding. It would be easier to walk away if Rafe had shunned her, but he hadn't.

Ten years with the fae queen had changed her. Rafe had been there for her, comforting her through the dark nights. And it was always the night that brought out her demons. He was the only one, besides her sisters, whom she trusted. Before she knew it, he had charmed himself right into Adaira's heart, which only angered her. He wasn't supposed to fall in love with her. He'd melted away her fears and loved her with an undeniable passion. Even now, as angry as she was with him, she longed to feel his warm breath against her ear, assuring her there was nothing to fear.

Rafe made it too easy to want to live in the light, to love him back.

Her heart felt like someone had reached into her chest and squeezed it as she thought about a life without Rafe. She'd never be right for him. She was incapable of loving Rafe in a way he needed—the queen had made sure of that. The queen always took those who she dared to love away. Besides, the monster inside her didn't deserve a man like Rafe.

Aye, he was in close proximity of her heart. She was in trouble.

Adaira opened her eyes. Flurries danced like fairy fire falling from the sky. She looked up at the stars and moon, hopeful one would fall. Before she knew it, she had a wish fresh on her tongue just like the night she had changed her fate.

"Leana, where are ye, lass?"

She didn't know why she watched for a falling star, for wishing upon a star had only brought her trouble, yet she was desperate. Adaira had to find Leana. If anything bad happened to her sister, she'd never forgive herself.

She rested her head against the wall and fell asleep.

She awoke, but wasn't in the bedchamber. She was in the forest, crouched behind a tree spying on three men. Spying? Nay, hunting. They were handsome, no more than eight and ten, and looked travel-weary. Unfortunately for them, wandering too close to the fairy mound made them perfect prey.

Adaira ran a few yards ahead so the lads would cross her path. She adjusted her breasts so they were accentuated just enough to catch their eyes in her tight bodice. She arranged her hair over her shoulders. Aye, no mere mortal could resist her. She grabbed her basket and stepped out of the shadows.

It wasn't long before the lads reached her.

"Pardon me," one said. "Would ye know where the nearest village is?"

Adaira stood from picking nuts off a hazel bush. "Och, ye startled me."

They stared at her in awe.

One finally spoke, "I—I dinnae mean to scare ye, lass. We've been traveling for days and have run out of food. Can ye point us in the direction of the nearest village?"

Adaira averted her gaze. "I'm terribly sorry. I must go." She turned around to leave when one of the boys grabbed her hand.

"Please, we will no' harm ye. We are hungry."

Me, too. She hid her wicked smile before turning back around.

"We'd be most grateful." He pulled a small, black pouch from his tunic.

Adaira took the offering and looked inside. Coin. She eyed the lads. "What makes ye think I know where the nearest village is?"

"We have no' seen a soul out here for days. Ye must have come from somewhere."

"Aye, in my dreams." The larger of the three said as he stepped forward. "Me name is Alex." He bowed. "These are me brothers, Thomas and Kenneth."

She giggled, pretending to be flattered. "'Tis a pleasure. I'm Adaira. My village is no' far. Ye're welcome to follow me back for food and drink."

She led the sacrificial lambs through the forest. She could sense their hesitation—hear their rapid heartbeats, yet they kept following her. "My mother is working at the tavern today. She'd be delighted to prepare provisions for ye," Adaira said over her shoulder.

"How much longer?"

"Just past the clump of rowan trees." Adaira pointed straight ahead.

She escorted them inside the tavern. "Have a seat." Adaira placed her basket on the table.

"Brother," Kenneth whispered to Alex." I do no' have a good feeling about this. "Look inside the basket."

Alex hovered over the basket. "Adaira, if ye were picking nuts why is yer basket empty?" He looked up, and Adaira met him with a grin.

"Sit." Adaira stared deeply into his eyes. "I'll go tell mother we have guests."

Entranced, Alex nodded and sat at the table.

Seconds later, Adaira returned with her two sisters.

"I can no' believe me eyes," Alex said. "There's three of them."

"Aye." Adaira continued to play along. "This is Leana and Masie. They are my sisters."

Leana and Masie smiled, deepening their spell on the lads. "We thought we could keep ye company while ye eat," Masie said and placed a bowl of stew on the table before Kenneth.

"Aye." He stood and pulled out a chair for Masie. "I'd be daft to turn away such beauty."

They sat while the brothers ate. Adaira kept their tankards filled with mead, and before long, their guests were drunk.

A harp began to play. "Where is the music coming from?" Alex asked.

Adaira stood and offered her hand to him. "Dance with me." She smiled.

He couldn't resist her magic and joined her in a seductive dance.

It wasn't long before everyone was dancing.

"It's time," Adaira finally said.

"Aye," Leana agreed. "I'm hungry."

A gust of wind blew into the tavern causing the tapers to flicker and blow out.

"What the devil?" Alex exclaimed as he frantically looked around the room.

"I told ye something was wicked here," Kenneth said.

"Aye." Adaira whispered in Alex's ear. "Yer observations are correct."

He tried to latch onto her, but she vanished.

The tapers flashed into blazing torches. The lads stood back-to-back in the center of the room watching the tavern transform into something they'd never seen before. The floor creaked as blackthorn branches sprouted from the ground.

Adaira smelled their fear as the spikey vine weaved closer around them.

The brothers huddled closer together. "Dinnae touch the branches," Alex warned. "The spikes are poisonous."

The branches formed a tunnel. They couldn't see what or who stood at the end of it, but whatever it was, evil emanated from the other side.

Adaira came up behind them. "Dinnae be frightened wee lambs. She can smell yer fear."

Adaira and her sisters shepherded the lads through the tunnel until they reached a dark figure standing in the shadows.

A woman stepped into sight, and Adaira heard Alex gasp. She breathed in their bone-chilling terror, electrified by it. The anticipation before a kill was always exciting.

"My queen." The sisters bowed.

Queen Galanthus drifted toward the boys with two of her fae princes behind her. She stopped in front of Alex, took his chin in her hand, moving his head back and forth, inspecting the prey. "Yer strength is mighty." Her eyes raked down his neck.

The queen released him and continued to the next brother. "Aye, strong, young lads."

"Please, have mercy. We mean ye no harm." Alex's voice shook.

The queen turned and smiled at the princes standing behind her. "They want me to show mercy. I do consider myself gracious. And I reward those who show me loyalty. However, dear fools, ye could never give me what I seek. Therefore, ye mean nothing to me. Yer fate has been sealed."

"Please," Kenneth sobbed. "I beg ye to let us go. I'll tell no one."

"Brother, do no' show these creatures weakness," Alex warned.

In the blink of an eye, the queen was mere inches from Alex's face, placing her long, boney finger over his lips. "Shh. Take heart, *all of ye are providing us with sustenance. 'Tis an honor to serve an Unseelie queen. Even more of one to feed her."*

Terror spread across his face. "I have heard of yer kind. Baobhan siths. Beautiful lasses who seductively lure travelers so they can eat them. I should have known this was trickery."

"No trickery. Ye came of yer own free will." The queen opened her arms. "Girls." She faced Adaira who was standing next to her sisters. "Yer reward awaits."

Each sister took a lad by the neck. The girls' strength and hunger overpowered them as each tore into their flesh, sucking the life force from the lads' veins.

Adaira awoke to the sound of her bedchamber door opening. Her heart skipped a beat when she saw Rafe standing in the doorway.

"Good morn," he said.

"I dinnae see the good in it if we're no' leaving today." She pushed off the wall and walked to the wash bowl next to the bed, splashing the nightmare from her eyes.

"The snow has stopped. We leave now," he said dryly, apparently still upset from last night.

"Now?"

"Aye, unless ye've changed yer mind."

"Nay. The quicker we make it back to Dornoch, the sooner I find out what happened the night of Beathen's murder."

Rafe shook his head.

"Ye promised to take me to Cormag."

"Ye don't have to remind me." He shoved his hands through his hair. Adaira could see how conflicted Rafe was about taking her to Dornoch. "I must be a fool."

"Rafe—"

"No, I don't want to hear anymore. There's no changing

yer mind. Be ready to leave." Rafe strode out of the bedchamber.

Adaira didn't know what to say or think. Rafe had never talked to her like that before. Had she pushed him too far this time?

9

RAFE LED the pack west where the mountains met the sea. Dornoch was still a long ride away, but they would make up for some lost time since the snow had stopped.

Rafe took in the salty air as he watched a flock of gulls fly overhead. Their high-pitched cries brought him peace which he desperately needed after last night's fight with Adaira. The stress was wearing on him. He was growing tired of lying to his pack. One slip, and he'd be found out. And the situation with his sister and Ranger only added more grief to his life. The Mad Dog paced inside him relentlessly.

With Seren and Teg gone, Rafe was left to guard Adaira. He didn't trust anyone else; at least that's what he told himself. He knew damned well why he didn't want another wolf around his woman. She was his to claim.

Rafe motioned for Ranger to take the lead as he rode back to check on Adaira. When they left the tavern, he'd noticed how her cheeks were slightly hollow. She was still weak from the fae poison. Rafe reached the iron cage and his heart sank. No matter how many times he reminded himself that she wasn't his prisoner, it killed him to see her kept like an animal. He should have never allowed her to persuade him into this daft plan of hers. Then again, Adaira was as stubborn as a mule. He had to go along with the plan to keep her safe.

"Aye, the mighty wolf leader," Adaira said as he approached. "Have ye come to make sure the blood sucker is behaving properly?"

"'Tis enough. I'm concerned. Ye look ill."

Adaira pulled her cloak around her shoulders. "I fare well."

Rafe knew she was hiding the truth. "I see ye've changed yer clothes."

"Aye, the lass from the tavern brought me a fresh gown and shoes before we left."

"That was generous of her."

"Aye. She wanted to thank Seren and me for saving her from Ranger's advances last night."

"What do ye mean?"

"If it was no' for yer sister, Ranger would have raped the young lass. I had to step in or Seren would have cut his throat."

Rafe thought about what he'd just heard. It all made sense. Ranger wasn't violent toward women. In fact, the way the wolf had handled his quarrel with Seren was out of character. Aye, they were forever arguing, and wolf law forbidden Rafe from getting involved. But now, knowing Ranger had made advances toward another woman, a woman who wasn't his mate, he could do something about it.

"Adaira, I'm sorry. I didn't know about Ranger's behavior last night. Is the lass well?"

"She's shaken up a wee bit. She'll be fine."

"I'll take care of this. Ye have my word."

"I hope yer word is better than wolf law," Adaira said dryly. "I'm more concerned about Seren. Will she come back?"

God's bones, the woman knew where to hit him. "Aye, we're her pack. She'll come home." He rode to the front of the line. Someone needed to be dealt with.

"Master Rafe," Ranger greeted him.

Rafe nodded. "I'll get straight to the point. Is it true? Tell me 'tis not." This wasn't easy for Rafe. He'd known Ranger for a long time and had never seen a more skilled warrior. Though the wolf liked to drink ale too much. After breaking up numerous drunken brawls, Rafe had warned him to stop drinking before it was too late. Unfortunately, it had gotten worse when Seren refused to honor their partnership.

"I don't understand what I'm supposed to say. Seren and I had a fight and..."

"That's not what I'm talking about. The lass from the tavern."

"Rafe, Seren had me roused from a previous fight. I admit I was drunk and foolish, but I..."

"Ranger, as yer Alpha, I must take action. Ye know the rules. I may not be able to get involved in what happened between Seren and ye, but I can punish ye for what ye did with the lass."

"I didn't hurt her or Seren. Ye must believe me."

"I'll believe what Seren tells me. And since she's not here to tell her side of the story, ye're banished from the pack until she returns."

"Ye can't do this to me."

"I've made my decision. Take this time to think about yer problems. Once I've talked to Seren, I'm sure we'll clear things up."

"Nay." Ranger halted his horse. "This has nothing to do with Seren. Ye're taking sides with a blood drinker."

"That's right. I said what everyone else is thinking but are too scared to say." Ranger dismounted and drew his sword. "Well, I'm not scared of the Mad Dog."

"Are ye challenging me?" Rafe dismounted. "I know ye're angry, but ye don't want to do this."

"Aye. I do." Ranger swung his sword, the tip grazing Rafe's cheek.

Stunned by Ranger's aggressiveness, Rafe wiped his face. He stared at the blood on his fingers. As much as he didn't want this to happen, Ranger had made it perfectly clear that he did. Rafe drew his sword. "I always knew yer ballocks were bigger than yer brains."

"Let's see what ye got, old man." Ranger lunged, bringing his sword over his head. The sharp edge slashed through Rafe's tunic as he dashed out of the way.

Rafe advanced. Their swords clanged together, sounding like claps of thunder. Rafe didn't want to hurt Ranger, he preferred to wear the wolf down until Ranger came to his senses. 'Twas his only hope at keeping the Mad Dog locked away. He didn't want to kill Ranger.

With all his might, Rafe came down hard with his sword, knocking Ranger's weapon from his hand. But it was too late. The Mad Dog was coursing through his veins. Rafe tossed his sword to the ground and ran toward Ranger, spearing him in the gut with his shoulder. They fell to the ground in a heap of swinging fists. Rafe straddled Ranger, firing off punch after punch to his head. He couldn't stop as he remembered the terrified look on Seren's face when he walked into her bedchamber last night. The bastard dared to hurt his little sister.

Rafe didn't know how long he'd been pounding away.

He wanted the bastard to bleed, to hurt the way he'd hurt Seren. It wasn't until one of his men pulled him off Ranger that he stopped.

"My lord," William warned. "Ye'll kill him."

Breathing hard, Rafe glared down at Ranger's bloody face. William held him back, for Rafe wasn't ready to call off the fight. "Are ye satisfied?"

Ranger slowly stood, spitting blood from his mouth. He didn't look at Rafe as he shifted into a wolf and ran into the forest with his tail tucked.

Rafe shoved away from William's grip. He wiped his mouth with the back of his hand, tasting blood from his cracked lip. "Bastard," Rafe snarled.

William handed him a water skin. "He was a fool to challenge ye, my lord."

Rafe took a gulp of water. "Aye." He walked back to his horse and mounted. The pack watched as he rode to front of the line. No one said a word. They followed their Alpha without complaint.

The terrain turned rugged and difficult for the horses to maneuver through safely. Rafe followed a narrow path to the shoreline. It was less traveled, but a shorter route. Rafe had been gone too long from home. He missed the salty taste in the air, the sound of the waves crashing against the rocky shore. But most of all, he missed the tranquility of the ocean. With his nose to the wind, he inhaled. Aye, there was nothing better.

He lost himself to the raging sea, forgetting about Ranger and their fight, and fantasized about Adaira. He wondered how much she saw of the Mad Dog. Even though the fight was mild, considering what he was capable of, he didn't want her seeing him like this. However, it had to be done. He could not stand down and allow Ranger to best him. An Alpha couldn't show any signs of weakness or he was replaced. If a wolf challenged him, it was his duty to put the wolf back into place. Order must be kept.

Night was approaching fast and they needed to make camp.

Once they reached an area with cliffs that would shield them from the wind, Rafe gestured for his pack to stop. "We'll camp here tonight."

Rafe dismounted, handing his reins over to his squire. He went to check on Adaira. He didn't like the way she'd looked this morn. She was curled up sleeping, using her cloak as a blanket. "Adaira."

She raised her head. "Are we home?"

Rafe opened the door. "Nay. We're setting up camp for the night." He took her hand and helped her down. She was so weak and pale. "Adaira, ye need to feed."

"Nay. I just need to—" Adaira fell into his arms.

Shite. Quickly, Rafe looked around making sure they weren't being watched. To his relief, the pack was too busy setting up camp to notice Adaira in his arms. He needed to find a secluded place where Adaira could rest away from his men. There had to be a cave within the cliffs.

As he searched the cliffs, he finally found a small opening. Rafe ducked inside the cave. The ground sloped down at first, then leveled.

He carefully sat Adaira down and walked deeper inside, making sure they were the only ones around. To the average man, it was black as night inside, but not for Rafe. With his keen eyesight, he had no problem seeing what might be lurking. Convinced they were alone, he walked back to Adaira. "We're going to need a fire. I'll be back. Stay here."

Too weak to move, Adaira nodded.

It wasn't long before Rafe returned and built a fire.

"Adaira, ye have to feed. I want ye to take my vein." Rafe sat next to her. "Please, do this for me."

"I can no' take yer vein. I will no' do it."

"Ye'll die. I will not have that on my conscience. Here." Rafe pulled his hair back, exposing his neck. "Take it."

Adaira wetted her lips. A shiver ran through his body as she placed her icy hand on the side of his neck. "Ye do understand what ye ask of me, aye?"

The intensity of her stare made him swallow hard. "Aye."

She leaned in, lightly brushing her lips against his neck. "I've never tasted wolf before," she whispered, nibbling his ear.

By the saints. Did he truly understand what was going to happen? Taking his vein wasn't the problem—it was the way she made his cock jerk to life when her lips touched his skin. Tamping down the need to claim her would be a true test of his willpower.

Adaira slid her tongue up his neck. "Ye taste good, Wolf."

Even through weakness, Adaira was in charge. It was like her to toy with him—see how far she could push him. "Adaira, quit playing games. Drink."

She cupped his cheek. He didn't need to see that her fangs had extended, he felt them pierce his skin. The bite stung at first, then softened to a dull throbbing pain. As her thirst deepened, the need to be inside her intensified to something he couldn't ignore. There were no words to describe what was happening. It felt like stars shooting across his body and bursting every time she drank deeper.

With a desperate urge, he settled her on his lap so she could straddle him. "God's bones," he hissed as he leaned his head back, surrendering. He grabbed her arse with both hands and squeezed. She moaned.

She slid her hand up his cheek and into his hair. She grabbed a fistful and pulled back, breaking her hold on his neck. Rafe opened his eyes and was shocked by the darkness swirling in her eyes.

"Ye are a bad wolf," she teased.

"Aye." He pressed his cock against her womanhood. "Ye bring out the beast in me." He trailed his hands up her arms to the back of her neck. He threaded his fingers through her hair, pulling her in to claim her lips, but she stopped him.

She rested her forehead against his. "Rafe, we can no' do this."

"Why not? This is what we do." He continued to pull her down into a kiss, but was stopped again.

"I know. It must stop." Adaira straightened. "I can no' keep running to ye every time I have a problem. Ye need to be free to love a woman who's deserving of yer love. I am no' that lass. I dinnae love ye."

Rafe couldn't believe what he just heard. She didn't love him? Those words cut deep. He stared at her for a moment, taking everything in. In a way, her confession shouldn't have shocked him. He'd told her time and time again that he loved her, yet not once had she ever said it back. Aye, this was them...it never changed. Just when he thought he'd broken through her defenses, she reminded him how impenetrable she truly was. *No more.*

"Aye." Rafe exhaled and moved Adaira off his lap. "What was I thinking?" Frustrated, he stood.

Adaira looked up at him. "Rafe—"

"No." He shoved his hands through his hair. "How

many times do I need to show ye I don't care about yer past? I've accepted ye for who ye are. But still, ye push me away."

Adaira stood. "I'm sorry."

"Sorry?" Rafe shook his head, unable to think straight. "Ye're the most stubborn lass I've ever met."

"I'm no' stubborn," Adaira lashed out. "Ye're just angry because I will no' lay with ye."

Adaira's words struck another nerve—he'd had enough. She knew damned well that wasn't true. "Have it yer way, lass." Rafe grabbed a piece of wood and lit the end of it over the fire.

"Where are ye going?" Adaira asked.

"I don't know," Rafe grumbled. "Going away from ye."

"Dinnae go." Adaira grabbed his arm.

He glared down at her, waiting to hear an apology. A confession of her true feelings was the only reason he'd stay. He'd grown tired of the chase, wondering when he'd finally be able to claim her heart. Every time she pushed him away, she chipped away at his resolve to keep trying to win her love. The lass was too damn stubborn to admit she cared for him.

Who was he fooling? She'd never say the words he longed to hear. Rafe ripped his arm free and wandered deeper into the cave.

Adaira stood speechless. Her heart plummeted into her stomach as she watched Rafe disappear. Had she finally crossed the line? Had she taken it too far, claiming he only wanted to bed her? It was a horrible thing to say. She knew Rafe better than that.

Adaira sat next to the fire, deep in thought. Why couldn't she allow Rafe into her heart?

Ye do no' know how to love.

Aye, it was true. Her heart was closed off, walled up tight. "Love's a fool's feeling," she huffed. How could she love a man when the things she'd done to innocent men were what nightmares were made of? Even though it had been a long time since she'd taken a life, the men in her past still haunted her.

Ye have never had a chance to be truly loved by a man.

The truth was always a bitter brew to swallow. Doughall and the queen had stolen that part of her life. Love for her sisters was the only thing she could protect against their evil. And the only way Adaira could live with herself was to block out love and compassion.

But Rafe has been there every step of the way.

Aye. Rafe was risking his life and pack for her family. He'd comforted her through dark times. He'd taken the pain away, yet she treated him horribly. By far, he didn't owe her loyalty, but she had it. And here she was pushing him away.

What are ye scared of, Adaira Keith?"

She hung her head. She wasn't scared of anything...at least, that's what she told herself. "Losing my heart forever," she whispered.

Shite! Her conscience was relentless. "Maiden, Mother, Crone," she sighed. She didn't need this distraction, she needed to get back to Dornoch. She needed to find Leana.

Feeling torn, she didn't know why she felt the urge to go after Rafe. Her soul sought his forgiveness. Adaira stood and lit a piece of wood, then took off in the same direction as Rafe. She had to make things right between them.

She snaked her way through the cave. As she reached the end of the winding path, it opened into a large pool of water. Light from the bottom of the pool cast a soft glow throughout the cavern. A green mist hovered over the surface. She knelt and touched the water; it was warm and inviting.

Adaira stood and looked around at the crevasses embedded deep within the rock walls. She was at the end of the cave, he had to be nearby. "Rafe," she called. *Where are ye?*

She stood and wandered to the other side of the pool to get a better look at a giant rock above the pool. It wasn't very high, but high enough that she couldn't climb it. As she got closer, she noticed Rafe lying on his back with his hands folded behind his head.

"Come down. We need to talk."

Rafe didn't answer.

And he had the nerve to call her stubborn. "Rafe, dinnae be a grumpy auld goat. Come down."

He didn't respond.

Adaira placed her hands on her hips. She didn't appreciate being ignored, then again, she deserved it. But that was beside the point, Rafe was coming down off that rock one way or another. She looked across the pool. On the lower side of the rock, opposite of Rafe, water spilled into the pool, giving Adaira an idea. Mayhap a swim would encourage the wolf off the rock. The water was indeed enticing.

She undressed slowly, keeping an eye on Rafe, waiting for him to notice what she was doing. Completely naked, she stood with her hands on her hips. "I'm no' wearing any clothes."

She heard a low, deep growl, but he didn't look at her. *Fine, have it yer way.* Adaira stepped into the pool. It was exactly how she'd imagined it, warm and soothing. She walked out until the water covered her chest. She looked up at Rafe. Still not a glance. She dipped down, making a splashing noise so Rafe would take notice. She emerged from the water, running her hands down her wet, slick hair. The water licked at the tops of her breasts as she stood. "The water is warm. Come join me."

The growl grew louder. Adaira smiled, her plan was working, or was it? Rafe hadn't moved off that damned rock. Adaira swam closer to his perch. "I promise to bite," she teased.

His stubbornness was frustrating. She couldn't stand it. Adaira splashed him. "Ye can no' stay mad at me forever."

He still ignored her.

She swam to the waterfall. Upping the stakes, Adaira positioned herself under the spray. It was shallower in this part of the pool, so when she stood, her upper body was exposed. The cold air hit her skin and her nipples hardened. She turned, facing Rafe as she seductively rubbed her arms and neck. "Ye dinnae know what ye're missing, Wolf." She continued to run her hands up and down her body. "And to think I came here to apologize. I must be daft."

She heard the splash, then felt the warmth of his naked body behind her. He cupped her breasts and rolled her pebbled nipples between his fingers, giving them a light squeeze. The sting shot straight to her core. "It took ye long enough."

He nuzzled her hair and inhaled. "Ye have something for me? An apology?"

The deep rumble of his voice reminded her of who she was dealing with—a wolf. Adaira turned around and took a step back so she could think clearly. "Aye." She gazed into his silver eyes. "I dinnae mean to accuse ye of such an act. And I should have never given ye a tongue lashing about yer pack's laws. I...I." She couldn't continue. Admitting she'd been wrong, saying it out loud, and realizing she'd hurt someone she cared for dearly, broke her heart. A tear, something that didn't happen too often, slid down her cheek.

Rafe gently wiped it away. "Say what's on yer mind, lass."

Adaira sucked in a shaky breath. "'Tis no' easy for me to love. 'Tis easier for me to push ye away than deal with the pain. For so long, I've had to protect meself. The queen made me do unthinkable things and the only way I could live with meself was to harden me heart. I'm sorry, Rafe. I'm no' capable of the love ye seek from me."

"I think ye're wrong. Yer heart brought ye here. If ye didn't care, ye wouldn't have come looking for me."

His words gave her pause, for he was right. "And after everything I've done to ye...I dinnae deserve ye."

"Adaira, ye're wrong. Ye do deserve love."

"Nay, no' after the things I've done." She shook her head.

He cupped her face. "Look at me. The past is the past. I'm still burying mine, but together we can get through it."

"Seren told me about yer wife and child. I'm so sorry."

Rafe lowered his hands. A grim expression spread across his face. "Seren never knows when to keep her mouth shut."

Adaira's brows creased. "If we're going to make things work between us, we need to be honest. If ye want me to confide in ye, ye need to do the same."

"Together? Ye and me? No games?"

Giving Rafe her heart scared her to death. Was she even capable of letting her guard down after years of not trusting anyone? Did she even know how to let him in?

"Adaira," Rafe warned.

Could she live without him?

Inside, she shuddered as he towered over her with his

smoldering gaze on her body. Water dripped from the ends of his long, dark hair and down his bronzed skin. She followed a droplet trail down the rigid muscles of his chest and abdomen with a finger, stopping when she reached his navel. She fisted her hand, fighting the urge to take his length in her hands. Tearing her eyes away from his magnificent form, she met his gaze. Lust burned in his silver eyes, yet he was holding back. She knew what he wanted to hear, but could she say the words and mean it?

"Why did the gods send me an angel?" she asked. "Me heart is too cold."

He didn't speak.

"Ye are the only one dark enough to see through the blackness in me heart." She caressed his whiskered cheek. "I can no' walk away from ye anymore, Rafe. I love ye."

Tears filled his eyes. "Ye have no idea how long I've waited to hear those words from ye. One thing that will never falter is my love for ye." He cupped the back of her neck, circling the nape with his thumb.

The warmth of his touch breathed life back into her cold heart. Aye, she really did love him.

He pulled her close and dipped his head until his lips brushed against hers. She inhaled, anticipating the kiss. Desire for this man burned away all her resolve. With a ravenous hunger, she claimed his mouth. His hands tangled in her hair as he pulled her in, deepening the kiss. Their tongues swirled together, reigniting an old flame she'd longed to feel again.

He walked her forward, taking her behind the waterfall. His big body pinned her against the cave wall. The cold rocks bit into her skin, but she didn't care. She wrapped her arms around his waist, tugging him closer. Her body ached for his touch. The problem was, she didn't know where she wanted him to begin. "I've missed ye, Wolf," she sighed against his ear.

"And I, ye." He nuzzled her neck, awakening another wave of desire as he wrapped her leg around his waist. The need for his touch consumed her as his cock pressed against her womanhood. She needed this man—she needed his hands all over her body.

As if he'd read her mind, he squeezed her arse cheeks. Adaira moaned, pressing her throbbing core against his hardened length. *By the saints, she'd missed this man.*

He slipped his fingers between her folds. Knowing his masterful touch, she bit her bottom lip as he teased her, grazing his finger up and down her hot, wet flesh. "Dinnae stop touching me," she sighed and rocked her hips forward.

Rafe growled and glided his finger deep inside her.

She gasped at the initial sting, then relaxed. He took her to the edge but stopped suddenly, withdrawing his fingers. She cried out, but in one powerful thrust, he buried his cock inside her.

"By the gods, Adaira..."

She gripped his shoulders, pressing her fingernails into his flesh as she felt him stretching her. She began to panic as the severity of her decision came crashing down on her. Her body tensed. *Push him away...protect yer heart.* She didn't know if she could completely give herself to Rafe. In the past, there was no threat of getting hurt, it was just sex. Or at least, that's what she had convinced herself to believe. It was different now. She couldn't push him away, nor did she want to.

Could she allow him access to the most vulnerable parts of her heart?

She had to put an end to this—for good. She pulled back. Rafe threaded his fingers through her hair and raised her head so she had to look at him. Tears ran down her cheeks. Her walls came back up—strong as steel.

"Adaira, stay with me in this moment."

"I...I dinnae think I can."

"Don't think...feel." He kissed her tears away.

She nodded and sucked in a shaky breath. *Feel.* She slowly exhaled. She repeated this a few more times, her fears retreating with each breath. Rafe's gentle touch melted away her doubt in love. She was worthy. She could do this, wanted to.

She leaned her head back, resting it against the wall. Rafe consumed her mind, body, and soul as they found a pleasurable rhythm. Heat washed over her body. Her legs trembled. She felt weightless. Holy hell, she was going to shatter.

"Stay with me, my heart's queen."

Wrapping her arms around his neck, she held on as her body began to hum with pleasure. The harder he pumped, the more she wanted to surrender.

"Rafe," she moaned and felt his body tense. She smiled as he growled, spilling his seed deep inside her.

He braced his arms against the wall. "Ye take my breath away, lass."

10

RAFE CRADLED his queen in his arms and sat down in the water, resting his back against the cave wall. He could stay here forever as long as Adaira was with him. "If this is a dream, I'll slay the bastard who wakes me."

Adaira giggled. "Aye, the poor bastard."

He kissed the top of her head. "Ranger has been banished from the pack until Seren comes home."

"I saw." She kissed his chest.

"How much did ye see?"

"Enough. I dinnae feel sorry for him. Seren will be wounded forever."

"I want to believe he's telling the truth. He said he was drunk and not thinking clearly when he groped the barmaid. I've warned him time and again he needed to stay away from the ale. God have mercy on his soul if he's hurt my sister."

"I'll never understand wolf law, but I hope the bastard stays far away from Seren. And I hope she'll come home soon. I like her."

"Adaira Keith openly admitting she likes someone... thought I'd never see the day," he teased.

Adaira smacked his chest playfully. "I have me moments."

The dark cloud that hovered over Rafe returned. By the evening meal, they would arrive at Dornoch, which meant Adaira was closer to her fate with Cormag. He couldn't imagine what the bastard had in store for her. He'd seen how the laird dealt with murderers. Hung, drawn, and quartered. To make matters worse, this crime was personal. Cormag would torture Adaira until he felt the vengeance over losing his son had been satisfied. Knowing firsthand what it was like to carry such bitterness, Rafe feared the worst. How was he going to protect her?

A shiver ran down his spine thinking of the ways Cormag would make Adaira pay. He held her close as she played with his chest hair. He trailed his fingertips up and down her arm. Everything he held dear in the world was in his arms. There was no way he could turn her over.

"My heart, I cannot let ye go to Dornoch."

Adaira sat up. "Rafe, I have to go back. 'Tis the only way to find out what truly happened."

"What if ye don't find anything? Or worse yet, what if ye learn that Leana killed Beathen? Do ye think the laird will grant ye freedom? He'll lock ye away until he finds Leana and make ye both pay for murdering his son. I cannot deliver the woman I love to her death. Please, Adaira, I beg ye to reconsider."

"Yer pack is growing suspicious. If I suddenly escape, they'll know someone betrayed the pack. The risk is far greater for ye than me. Besides, I can no' run from Cormag forever. At least if he has me, Leana is safe."

"Ye honor yer sisters well."

"They are all I have. In a way, I'm at fault for our misfortunes."

"Adaira." He tried to pull her close but she pushed away.

"Nay, Rafe. There was a part of Doughall ye didnae see. He was terrible to me mother and..." she swallowed. "He wanted a male heir in the worst way. When he'd given up on me mother, he forced me into an arrangement when I was ten and three. He ordered me to bear him a male heir. I was to marry a man of his choosing and conceive a child. He didnae tell me mother. I was to keep it secret."

"Wait...ye are married?"

"If ye call living in hell for a year marriage, then aye. The contract was valid for a year. If I gave birth to a son, then after a year and a day, the marriage was legal. If I did no' bear a son, then I was left with nothing but a tarnished reputation. Doughall cared more about the man I was to marry than his own daughter. Me father didnae want to burden me husband with a barren wife." Adaira hung her head. "I never want to see the bastard again."

"Adaira." Rafe lifted her head until their eyes met. "Ye're keeping something more from me. What is it?"

She took in a deep breath. "Doughall grew tired of me refusing me husband. Eventually, he stepped in and forced me to consummate the marriage. The man me father chose was cruel and much older than me. He raped me, broke me down until I submitted. And me father watched the whole thing. I tried to fight him off." Adaira crossed her arms over her chest. Tears welled in her eyes. "But he was too strong."

"Bastard," Rafe growled.

"When I returned to me bedchamber, Leana saw the bruises on me face, but I never told her what happened. I didnae have to. She sensed what was going on and desperately wanted Doughall to pay for hurting her family.

She took the blood oath with the fae queen because of me. If I had only stopped her, none of this would have happened."

"He's still alive?" Rafe prayed the man was, because he wanted to kill him for hurting Adaira.

"Aye. I mean, I think so."

"Which is it?"

"Why all the questions? I said the marriage is over. I dinnae care if the man breathes or no'."

"I do." He cupped her face. "Now I understand why ye stood up for Seren. Seeing her like that must have brought back horrible memories. But know one thing, lass, none of this is yer fault." He wrapped her in his arms, wishing he could take her pain away. Aye, if he'd known this side of Doughall, he would have cut the laird's ballocks off and fed them to the pigs, along with the man who dared touch his queen.

"Now ye understand why I must go back. I must prove Leana is innocent. 'Tis the only way I know how to protect her. I need to find her and bring her home before she turns to the queen for help again."

Rafe exhaled. "Aye, lass, I understand. I wish there was another way."

"I'll be in good hands. Ye'll be there to protect me."

"Aye, I'd risk my life for ye."

"And I love ye for that." Adaira pulled him down so she could kiss him. "I can handle Cormag. He does no' frighten me. He claims land that belongs to me. He has forgotten I'm the true laird of Clan Keith. He's picked a battle with the wrong lass."

Rafe grinned. "'Tis time for Dornoch's queen to come home and claim her throne."

Rafe was jerked out of the moment when he sensed

someone was watching them. The intruder cleared his throat.

Teg was standing with his arms folded across his chest. "Brother," Teg greeted, then nodded to Adaira. "I see I've caught ye at a bad time."

Quickly, Rafe stood with Adaira. She covered her breasts and hid behind Rafe. "Teg."

"Surprised to see me?"

Rafe was speechless. What was running through his brother's mind right now seeing him naked with Adaira?

"Ye should cover yer tracks better," Teg warned. "I could smell ye from the beach."

"Tegwyn, I can explain. Let me dress and we can talk."

"I'll wait outside." Rafe caught Teg's disapproving glare as he turned and headed out of the cave.

"Shite." Rafe hopped out of the water and quickly began to dress. Adaira followed.

"I'm so sorry. Will he tell the rest of the pack?" Adaira asked as she yanked her dress over her wet body.

Rafe cupped her face. "Don't worry."

"Dinnae worry? Rafe, if Teg tells anyone, ye'll be banished like Ranger."

"I know my brother. Everything will be fine." He kissed her. "Go sit by the fire. I'll be back soon." He turned to leave, but Adaira grabbed his arm.

"Come back to me, Wolf."

The urge to throw her over his shoulder and claim her again was a fleeting thought. He had business to settle with his brother. Rafe kissed her cheek and walked away.

"Is she worth it?" Teg was leaning against the outside of the cave, chewing on a blade of dead grass. "Is she?"

Rafe walked over to his brother. "I can explain."

"No," Tegwyn exclaimed. "I've had enough of living in

the shadows of the Mad Dog. I'm not about to live through that hell again. Ye told me Adaira and ye were over. Christ, Rafe, ye've been protecting the Keith sisters all along, haven't ye?"

Rafe grabbed Teg by his tunic and gave him a firm shake. Brother or not, he'd not let anyone threaten his future with Adaira. Especially after today, the lass loved him. "This has nothing to do with ye. Adaira and her sisters need my help."

"But we serve Laird Cormag, or have ye forgotten?"

"I know damned well who I serve. I've taken grave measures to make sure the pack will not be held responsible for my actions. If ye keep yer mouth shut, no one will know. I cannot turn my back on the woman I love."

"Ye're turning yer back on the pack. Please," Teg pleaded. "I cannot go through life without ye. If the pack finds out ye've betrayed their trust, they will rip ye limb-from-limb. We're family. The woman isn't worth the risk."

"Hold yer tongue," Rafe warned.

"I will not stand by and watch the Mad Dog return when she rips yer heart out."

Rafe paused. He knew what troubled Teg. Hell, it haunted him as well. The night Rafe had gone rogue and murdered the wolf hunters was still a fresh memory for Teg. His brother had witnessed it all, the bloodshed and his ultimate fall from grace. Aye, Teg had carried the burden of being the Mad Dog's brother.

"Brother." Rafe clasped the back of Teg's neck. "I cannot begin to understand what ye've been through because of me. I am truly sorry, but I'm not the same wolf I once was. Trust in me. I will never do anything to harm ye or the pack. I love Adaira, and if the devil stood in my way, I'd battle him to the death if it meant keeping her safe."

Teg straightened. "Is she worth losing yer life for?"

"Aye."

It was apparent this wasn't easy for Teg to accept. "Ye have my loyalty. I will not say a word."

Rafe pulled Teg into a hug. "I've never doubted ye, Brother."

"Aye." Teg pulled out of his embrace. "What's the plan?"

"We're returning to Dornoch so Adaira can clear her sister's name."

"That's madness," Teg exclaimed. "Cormag will kill her before dawn."

"Not if I can help it."

"I don't like the sound of this."

"'Tis the only way Adaira can find out who murdered Beathen."

"Do ye believe the girls are innocent?"

Rafe averted his gaze.

"Brother? What are ye not telling me?"

"Adaira was with me the night of the murders. She claims Masie saw Leana with Beathen and another lad. There were puncture wounds on their necks."

"Shite."

"Adaira believes Leana is innocent, but she has to prove it to Cormag."

"Bringing Adaira back to Dornoch is too risky. Cormag is sick with revenge. He'll make her pay whether she's guilty or not. Have ye another plan?"

"Nay. However, Doughall and Cormag were close. The laird cannot do anything rash since she's a Keith. My plan is to get Adaira to the blacksmith shop quickly so she can search for clues, then take her far away from Dornoch."

"What if ye're caught?"

Rafe grinned. "Ye worry too much."

"Ye don't worry enough."

Rafe rolled his eyes.

"What?" Teg asked.

"Where were ye?"

Teg shifted on his feet. "I picked up an unusual scent back at camp. I followed it to the glen. It was unlike anything I've smelled before. It was sweet, yet foul."

Rafe's heart skipped a beat. "Sweet and foul?"

"Aye"

"Where did the scent lead ye?"

Teg shoved his hands through his hair as he continued. "That's just it, I don't remember."

"What do ye mean ye don't remember?"

"One moment I was running through the woods, the next I woke up inside a cottage with bandaged ribs." Teg pulled up his shirt. "I believe I was being chased, but cannot remember a thing except for that scent."

"So, ye weren't tracking Leana?"

"Nay. I thought it was her at first, but it wasn't."

If Rafe's instincts were right, the smell Teg described sounded like fae. "Teg, don't hunt alone. There's fae trickery here."

"The fae?"

"Aye. They're after Adaira."

"Holy hell, Brother. What have ye brought upon us? First Cormag, now the fae."

Rafe's jaw tightened as he thought about the fae hurting his brother. "Just be on guard."

"Aye."

Rafe headed back into the cave with a heavy heart. The queen had found Adaira.

11

QUEEN GALANTHUS SAT on her throne made of twisted blackthorn branches. Lost in deep thought, she stared into the flames burning inside a shallow iron bowl hanging from the ceiling. The Keith girls had deceived her and broken their blood oath with her when they left. However, since her blood now flowed in their veins, they couldn't hide forever.

She'd been well-advised of the sisters' whereabouts and called forth brutal winter storms in the hope of slowing their escape. But her efforts were for nothing. They were more resourceful than she'd given them credit for.

"They'll be back."

She stood and walked over to the window where a basket of snowdrop blossoms hung. She waved her hand over the bell-shaped flowers and they began to glow. Energy flowed from her fingertips to the petals and down their narrow leaves. She picked one.

The snowdrop was the only flower that grew in the winter. It was resilient yet delicate—pure like fallen snow, just like her Masie. She gripped the petals. "Masie, come home." She clutched the snowdrop tighter, inflicting pain on Masie. Wherever she was, she'd feel pain beyond compare.

She opened her hand and watched the crumbled remnants of the flower float through the air. To her surprise, the blossom took its shape again before hitting the ground. Something was blocking her magic. She picked the flower up and examined it closely.

The doors to her chamber flew open and she turned to see one of her dark princes approaching her with haste. "My queen."

His sudden interruption wasn't welcomed. The queen glared at him. She needn't say a word; her servants were forbidden to enter unbidden. "Ye'll address yer queen properly." Galanthus deepened her stare. Unwillingly, the prince fell to his knees and bowed his head.

"Forgive me, yer majesty."

"Ash." She ran her fingers through his long, black hair. "My son, my orders were to bring Adaira to me. What happened?"

He stared at the ground. "She outran me."

The queen laughed. "Ye dare lie to me, child?" She yanked his head back so she could look him in the eyes. "I see everything."

"I was called back before I found her, my queen. I thought ye had sent for me."

She released him. "I did no such thing."

She returned to her throne and tapped her fingernails on the wood, deep in thought. First, someone was blocking her magic, and now, someone had summoned her prince home without her permission.

Startled from her thoughts, she stood and watched as her other two princes dragged a woman into her chambers. "My queen." They bowed their heads.

Her blood boiled when she realized who her servants had captured.

"We found her in the glen."

"Alder, Aspen." She nodded in appreciation. "My sons, ye have brought me a treasure. Ash, ye may join yer brothers."

The three princes stood shoulder-to-shoulder as the queen studied them. They were beautiful creatures, the finest Unseelies she had ever seen. She loved them as her own children. The princes guarded her kingdom, and for that, they were considered trusted advisors.

She turned her attention to the woman. "All these years I thought ye were dead, Sister."

"I'm no' dead."

"That's obvious. What brings ye here? Have ye missed me?" The queen smirked.

"I've come to make sure ye will never harm my daughters again."

"Dearest sister, ye were forever the dreamer." She laughed. "And how will ye accomplish such a bold task?"

"Take me. I'll do yer bidding. In return, ye'll leave me daughters alone."

The queen considered her sister's offer. "A blood oath can never be broken. The deal was made. Doughall is dead. I just happened to gain three lives for the price of one. Mayhap, ye should have been a better mother to them."

"They were wee ones. Ye took advantage of their innocence," Helen cried.

"They wanted to change their fates and I helped them like a good aunt would."

"Galanthus, how did ye become so cruel?"

The queen grabbed Helen's chin. "When ye stole Doughall's heart."

"It was no' me fault. He kidnapped me on me wedding day. I didnae love him. The only good thing that came out of our marriage were me daughters. I should have left Doughall long before me girls sought ye out."

"Do ye expect me to show ye pity? Before Doughall set eyes on ye, he loved me. Ye ruined everything." The queen studied her sister, remembering her own youth. "I was once like ye, Sister." She ran her fingers through Helen's hair, thinking how much Leana looked like her mother. "I was a kind, loving Seelie fae who was good at heart."

"Galanthus, ye can still be. Redeem yerself. Release me daughters. I'm here to take their place. Please, we were close once. Remember, in the spring when we'd pick wildflowers for Mother?"

Aye, she had been happy once. Frolicking through the glen and dancing around the fairy mounds with her sister were happy memories she'd never let go. Their mother was a beautiful Seelie fae and their father had been an immortal, Pictish warrior, a god to his tribe. She smiled. "Blue flowers were mother's favorite."

"Aye. Dinnae ye want to feel the sun warm yer skin again? This dark, Unseelie world is no' what ye want. Is it?"

The reflection of a happier time faded into blackness. "That was long ago. Besides, ye don't know me at all. Ye never really did. Why would I give up the kingdom I've built just so I can feel the sun again? I'm the queen and it's good to be queen."

"Dinnae let Doughall come between us. He should pay, no' my daughters."

"Oh, sweet sister, Doughall has paid dearly already. I am true to my word. As far as yer daughters are concerned, ye should have been honest with them. Keeping their true nature from them is inexcusable. Ye should thank me for unbinding them from yer spell."

"They are no' like ye. They are pure."

"*Were.* They are forever bound to the dark Unseelies. There's nothing I can do to change that. The girls will come home and ye'll see for yerself how much they have changed. Now, what to do about ye." The queen tapped her chin. "They say to keep yer enemies close. Ye'll serve me at court until further notice." The queen turned back to her throne. "Alder," she called over her shoulder. "Show our guest to her room. She's to stay there."

"As ye wish." Alder bowed.

"Sister, please."

"Take her away," the queen exclaimed as she took her seat. The queen's servants dragged her sister out of the chamber. A smile crept over Galanthus's lips as Helen begged for mercy. She now had the one thing that would bring the girls home, their mother. Soon, the whole family would be under her control.

12

THE HONOR GUARD reached the gatehouse of Dornoch before sunset. Two of Cormag's guards met Rafe in the bailey as he dismounted.

"Good evening," Rafe greeted them.

"The laird is waiting." One of the officers pushed him toward the cage that held Adaira. Rafe resisted, shoving the bastard back. "Go on. Open it."

"If ye're in that much of a hurry, then open the damn cage yerself." Rafe dangled the key in front of him. When the man refused the key, Rafe glared at him, stepping toe-to-toe with the guard "Are ye afraid?"

The guard looked away. "The laird doesn't like to wait."

"Coward." Rafe spat as he walked toward the cage.

Adaira gave him an encouraging look as he unlocked the door. He wished he could change her mind, all of this was much too risky.

Adaira stepped down. Rafe grabbed her arm and whispered, "Be on yer best behavior, lass."

She smiled.

Rafe shook his head. May the gods be with him today.

The officers escorted them inside the castle. Rafe's heart thundered as they entered the great hall where Cormag and his wife were sitting. All his wolf instincts warned him not to do this. His wolf wanted to be released so he could protect his mate.

Adaira bumped him with her shoulder and he looked down at her. "Dinnae worry yerself."

Rafe nodded for her sake. However, he wouldn't rest until they found the real murderer.

Rafe bowed to Cormag. When he realized Adaira was still standing, he tugged her arm and motioned for her to show respect. He glared at her when she refused to do as he wished.

Adaira's brows creased with anger. "I will no'."

"Do it," he bit back.

She rolled her eyes and bowed.

Rafe peered up, making sure the laird hadn't noticed their exchange. To his surprise, the laird's attention was on his wife. He gave Adaira a sideways look. "Yer stubbornness is going to get ye killed."

"Ye need to relax, wolf. I've battled far worse demons than this auld goat."

The laird motioned for everyone to stand. "Commander Rafe," his voice echoed through the great hall. "Come forward."

The officers stepped aside as Rafe approached the laird.

"Ye have served me well."

The laird stood and walked over to Adaira. He backhanded her, sending her to the floor. Rafe stifled a growl and fisted his hands, resisting the urge to rip the laird apart.

Adaira stood, pinning Cormag with a dark stare. Blood

trailed down the corner of her mouth where'd she'd been struck.

"Ye and yer sisters have caused me great grief. Me son dinnae deserve to die."

"Me laird, I'm deeply sorry for yer loss. Beathen was a good man. However, ye are greatly mistaken. We dinnae kill him."

"Dinnae dishonor me family with yer lies. I'm no fool. I know what ye are."

"I would never believe ye a fool, me laird. All I ask is to be treated fairly. Let me find the real murderer and bring him to justice."

Cormag laughed. "Why should I trust ye?

"There was a time ye pledged yer loyalty to me father. Ye swore to protect his family—this clan. I am the eldest daughter of the late Laird Doughall Keith. The warrior who fought for our lands."

"I dinnae need to be reminded. I fought alongside yer father. I paid for this life with sweat and blood on the battlefield."

"I respect yer loyalty to me father and clan. 'Tis why I never claimed me father's seat when he died."

"Everyone thought ye were dead." Cormag blew out a frustrated breath.

Adaira stepped closer. "Me sisters and I would never do anything to shame our clan, let alone commit murder. Ye welcomed us back when we returned home."

"A mistake I'll never make again."

"Please, I beg ye to believe me. Leana dinnae kill Beathen. The real killer is still out there."

Rafe cleared his throat. "My laird, may I speak?"

"Aye."

"I believe Adaira has a point. What would they have to

gain by killing Beathen? Nothing. Someone could be out there trying to gain yer attention. An enemy. We cannot ignore the possibility of a threat to our clan."

"Or maybe I have the real killer standing in front of me."

"Husband." Laird Cormag's wife stood. "Ye owe it to our son to find the person responsible for this heinous crime. Let Adaira prove her sister's innocence, for the sake of our son's memory."

Cormag faced his wife.

"Doughall would have done the same for ye." His wife joined him in front of Adaira. "Ye're filled with vengeance and 'tis interfering with yer good judgment. These girls are no' our enemies."

Cormag nodded, considering his wife's words. "Nay, the curse stops now. I will no longer stand by and watch the Keith sisters hurt our family." Cormag turned back to Adaira. "Ye can blame yer mother for that. She drove yer father to madness. Ye'll burn for the death of me son, and I will no' stop until every one of ye are dead."

The air in Rafe's lungs seized. This was exactly what he was afraid of. He should have never brought Adaira back here—a mistake he had regretted the moment he agreed to it.

"Guards, lock her in the south tower," Cormag ordered.

Adaira struggled to break away from the guards. "This is no' justice, Cormag."

"Be thankful I didnae send ye to the dungeons to rot."

Rafe watched as Adaira was dragged from the hall. He wanted to protect the woman he loved. Every fiber of his being urged him to rip Cormag's head from his body, but he couldn't—it would endanger his pack and Adaira.

"Commander Rafe, any word on the other sister?"

"Leana?"

"Aye."

"Nay, we haven't been able to pick up a scent."

"If ye value yer place here at Dornoch, ye'll find the girl and bring her to me. Have yer men readied and dinnae come back until ye've found her." The laird handed Rafe a small bag of coins. "As promised." Rafe grabbed the bag but the laird held on to it. Cormag pulled Rafe toward him. "Me eyes are on ye, Mad Dog. Ye'd be wise no' to disappoint me." He shoved the coins into Rafe's chest, then walked away.

With more force than he meant to unleash, Rafe came down with his sword, colliding with Tegwyn's. All morning they'd been sparring. It had been two long days since he last saw Adaira and it was driving him mad. He'd searched for a way to see her, but the tower was heavily guarded.

Teg shoved Rafe back a few steps. "Brother," he panted. "I'm not the enemy."

Rafe impaled the ground with his sword. His jaw tightened as he thought about Adaira being locked away like a criminal. "Forgive me, Teg. My mind is elsewhere."

His brother rested his hands on the hilt of his sword in front of him. "Ye haven't been granted access to Adaira?"

Rafe shook his head. "Nay, she's heavily guarded. The bastard laird thinks she has cursed the clan. Can ye believe the madness?"

"Shite, cursed?"

"Aye, she's been falsely accused and can do nothing but allow Cormag to get away with it. I swear with the gods as my witness, I'll find a way to free her. Then I'll gut Cormag."

"Careful, I hear the Mad Dog barking."

Rafe eyed Teg. "Mayhap, the beast should come out."

Those were strong and dangerous words. The urge to storm Cormag's bedchamber and slit his throat in the middle of the night was a thought that had played out over and over in his mind. He could even taste the laird's blood on the tip of his tongue.

"That look on yer face scares me," Teg said. "Are we going to battle?"

"Battle?"

"Aye," Tag said. "Why would there be any question about it? Adaira needs our help."

Rafe's brows creased. "Why do ye care about what happens to Adaira?"

"I know I've been harsh toward her in the past. But I see the way ye look at her. Ye love her, which makes her family."

Rafe shook his head. "Nay, this is my fight. I want ye to lead the pack now. Take them far away from here and start a new life. I cannot allow any more bloodshed."

Teg looked shocked. "I cannot believe what I'm hearing. Have ye forgotten that we live and fight together? Trust in yer pack, Brother. Don't break away from yer family. A lone wolf is a dead wolf."

"My decision is final." Rafe began to walk away.

"Don't go." Teg grabbed his arm. "The pack needs ye. I have felt a change coming on for a long time. Our people have grown tired of serving the laird like dogs. 'Tis time we make a stand. Let's take back this clan for Adaira. She's the rightful heir."

"I'd watch yer tongue. Clan Keith has been good to us when no one else was."

"Aye, but it was for their benefit, not ours. They use us. What do ye think will happen when the laird grows tried of us?"

Rafe yanked his arm free from Teg's grip. Everything his

brother said was true. He'd sensed it in the air and seen it on his men's faces. No longer would he look the other way and allow Cormag power over him. 'Tis best for his people to leave. He'd finish off Cormag. Adaira would be free and so would his pack. "Brother, I cannot allow the pack to stay and fight. Lead them to safety."

"With all due respect, I'm not asking for yer approval. We fight together." Teg pushed by him.

"I will not bring the pack into this matter," Rafe called after his brother.

"We are already involved."

"Ye're as stubborn as Seren."

"Aye, and prettier." Teg turned around and wriggled his brows at Rafe.

Rafe scratched his chin. Why was the laird so quick to condemn Adaira? Rafe thought about what his brother had said about Adaira being the rightful heir. There was something more here than justice for Beathen. If his suspicions were right, Cormag wanted to eliminate any threat to his seat as chieftain. And Adaira was the biggest threat.

The great hall was full of laughter, the savory aroma of cooked meat and pleasing music had put everyone in a good mood. It made Rafe's gut turn knowing what they were celebrating. In the last two days, hatred for the Keith sisters had grown. The laird held meetings, reassuring his people that he'd caught his son's murderer. He'd increased the bounty on Leana's head. Groups of hunters had left the castle in search of the girl so they could collect the reward.

With everyone distracted, now was the time to free

Adaira. Rafe would help her prove her innocence, and then he would deal with Cormag, alone.

Rafe made his way toward the back of the room where his pack sat together at a table. He walked up to Teg. "Tegwyn—"

"Come, sit," William, one of Rafe's oldest and most trusted mentors, interrupted. "We need to talk."

Rafe eyed Teg suspiciously. *What was he up to?*

"It has come to my attention ye wish Teg to lead the pack," William said.

"Aye." Rafe cleared his throat and clasped his hands together on the table. "I see Teg has informed ye of the situation. I have been dishonest. I've been secretly helping the Keith sisters escape Laird Cormag."

"'Tis about time someone stood up to that bastard," William said.

Rafe gave Teg a sideways glance. Teg shrugged.

"There's more here than Adaira's alleged crime. I believe the laird isn't after justice. He feels if Adaira or her sisters are alive, then his seat as chieftain is threatened. I must help her escape and prove her innocence. I don't expect the pack to get involved. As I told Teg, it's too risky. I want him to lead ye to safety and let me deal with Cormag. I don't expect, nor deserve yer loyalty."

William leaned forward. "Neither does Cormag. Love is a much greater force than a man seeking vengeance."

"William—"

"Let me finish. 'Tis true, we no longer want to be under Cormag's rule. Ye are our leader, our Alpha. We are loyal to ye. If battle is the only way to free us from the laird and save yer woman, then ye have my sword."

"I cannot ask that of ye."

"Have ye lost faith in yer pack, young pup? They may

outnumber us ten-to-one, but our wolves are more powerful."

Rafe exhaled and looked down the table. Hope shined in their eyes. There was no talking them out of it. They wanted their independence from Cormag. "William, do ye understand what ye're turning down? Ye can start a new life without the Mad Dog sullying yer name."

William emptied his tankard of ale and wiped his mouth with the back of his hand. "And leave all the fun for ye? Bah, we stay and fight proudly with the Mad Dog. Now, let's get ye inside that tower."

Rafe nodded. He couldn't force the words of gratitude past the lump in his throat. No matter what, this pack stayed together.

13

ADAIRA BLEW a stray hair out of her eye. She'd spent the better part of the day scraping away pieces of stone that secured the iron bars to the lone window in her room. Her fingernails were broken and her fingertips were bloodied, but she continued to claw away for her freedom. It was the only way out.

Her hand slipped and slammed into one of the iron bars. Pain shot down her wrist as her skin blistered from contact with the iron. "Shite," she hissed and held her hand to her chest. Defeated, she sat under the window, resting the back of her head against the wall. As she looked around the chamber, she was amused at how well Cormag had shut her in.

In addition to being heavily guarded, the room reminded her of a tomb. The curved walls were pure stone and the wooden door was reinforced with iron bars. Adaira chuckled. The bastard knew iron was the only thing that could keep her inside.

Tears stung her eyes. Two moons had passed—where

was Rafe? Had he deserted her? Was this his way of punishing her?

Maiden, Mother, Crone, she was slipping right back into old habits—second guessing Rafe's love and loyalty.

Rescuing her meant he had to continue to lie to his pack. Mayhap, she wasn't worth Rafe losing his family over. She exhaled. She should have known—to wolves, family always came first.

Adaira hugged her knees to her chest. The fight within her was beginning to fade. She was tired and hungry. Without her sisters, the isolation alone was playing tricks on her. Her body wanted to give up, and her mind wasn't far from its breaking point.

Her mother's voice echoed inside her head, "Courage does no' always roar. Be brave and try again tomorrow."

Adaira sniffled and wiped a tear from her cheek. *Leana needs me.* She looked at her hand as the last blister disappeared; her ability to heal quickly was something she appreciated. She made a fist, then opened her hand. Her fingertips were healed, her nails stronger than before. Aye, it was her duty as the eldest to keep her sisters safe.

Feeling pity for herself didn't suit her. That kind of thinking would only slow her down. She wasn't defeated. Cormag had no idea who he was dealing with.

Adaira had gone back to scraping the stone when the door swung open. She turned around and charged the door, showing her fangs.

"Easy, lass!" Rafe threw his hands up. "Adaira, it's me, Rafe."

The sound of his voice settled her restless spirit. She stood in front of him, hesitant to believe her eyes. "Rafe?"

"Aye, my queen."

She threw her arms around him, squeezing his neck. "What took ye so long?"

"I got to ye as fast as I could."

Adaira stepped out of his embrace. Rafe grabbed her shoulders and looked her over. "Are ye hurt?"

Adaira shook her head.

He cupped her face and kissed her. The taste of mint and spice exploded inside her mouth. *Rafe.*

She began to pull away, but was soon stopped as Rafe shoved his hands through her hair, keeping her in place so she couldn't break the kiss. He edged her backward with his big body, shutting the door behind him. He cupped her breasts. By the saints, she'd missed her wolf.

"Rafe," she said breathlessly. "As much as I want ye right now, we must stop."

Rafe growled against her neck and it sent a shiver down her spine. "I hate it when ye're right."

Adaira took a step back. "Wait, how did ye get past the guards?"

"I had some help," he winked.

"Yer pack knows about us?"

"Aye, and I'll explain everything. But first, we must get ye to the blacksmith shop. We don't have a lot of time."

Adaira nodded. "Aye."

Rafe opened the door and whistled. He waited. A second later, another whistle sounded. He looked back at Adaira. "We go now."

Adaira held his hand and followed him out of the chamber. They weren't far from the stairs. Halfway down, Adaira tripped into Rafe. His body stopped her fall. As she regained her balance, she saw what she'd tripped over. A dead guard propped against the wall with a broken neck.

Rafe looked back at Adaira. "Are ye all right?"

"Aye. I see how ye stormed the tower."

"The bastard won't stand between me and my queen again." He kissed her cheek. "Be careful and watch yer step."

Adaira smiled. "Aye."

As Adaira continued down the stairs, she sidestepped more bodies. She hadn't realized just how many men had been guarding the tower. Blood dripped from one step to another. The copper tinged smell of fresh blood caused her gums to throb. Her gut to tighten. *Resist the urge,* she warned herself.

Finally, they made it out.

Two of Rafe's men were disposing of the bodies in the woods. Adaira watched. There had to have been at least twenty dead men. Body parts littered the ground. She'd never seen a slaughter quite like this before. Aye, she'd seen dying men on the battlefield. However, this was different. These men had died *because* of her.

"Adaira." Rafe's concern was evident in his tone.

Knowing Rafe, he was worried about her witnessing the aftermath of a wolf battle. However, she felt no pity for these bastards. They should have run when they saw the wolves coming. To her, this was the price paid for choosing the wrong side to fight for.

"Yer pack did this? For me?" Adaira asked.

"Aye. They like Cormag as much as ye do."

"Wolf, I'm impressed and honored they would fight for me."

Rafe took her hands in his. "They think of ye as family."

"And why is that?"

"Because ye're mine." He caressed her cheek. The coarseness of his skin gave her gooseflesh.

Adaira shook her head. "I dinnae deserve such loyalty."

"We have an eternity to debate that point. Right now, we must go. We need to get ye to the blacksmith shop."

"Aye."

They sneaked their way through the bailey to the shop which was a few yards away. Adaira's heart began to race the closer they got. *The dreaded smithy.* Aye, part of her was a wee bit afraid of what she'd find inside. What was even harder to take was facing her past, a man she loathed and a name she vowed never to say again for as long as she lived.

She followed Rafe behind the forge wagon in front of the shop. They crouched down and stayed hidden.

"Let's go," Rafe urged.

She panicked and grabbed his arm.

"What's wrong?"

Words escaped her. She couldn't force herself to go inside.

"Adaira." Rafe squeezed her hand. "Look at me. What's wrong?"

She inhaled and closed her eyes, trying to ward off visions of the blacksmith. Her sister needed her to be strong. Adaira drew strength from Rafe's presence. "Auld ghosts," she said.

Rafe nodded. "I'll go in first. Ye stay put until I come for ye."

Adaira nodded, though reluctant to let him go.

"No one will harm ye ever again." He kissed her hand. "Ye have my word."

His intense gaze made her stomach flutter with desire and filled her heart with happiness. Rafe was risking his life for her family. All he wanted in return was her love.

Love? Was this what love felt like? She cupped his cheek and smiled tenderly. "I know, Wolf. Never would I have doubted it."

Rafe kissed her quickly. "Listen for my whistle."

"Aye."

Adaira watched Rafe slip closer to the smithy. He shouldered the door open and disappeared inside. She kept her eyes locked on the door while taking slow, steady breaths as she awaited his signal. She hoped she would find what she was looking for. Whatever it was, she prayed Leana was innocent. If not, she didn't know what to do. They couldn't keep running. The madness had to stop.

Rafe's shrill whistle sounded. She ran inside where Rafe waited with a lit torch. "I searched the shop. No one is here."

Relief washed over her. She wouldn't have to face the blacksmith.

"Do ye want me to wait outside?" Rafe asked.

"Nay." She looked around the dimly lit room. "Just keep an eye out for the blacksmith."

"Aye. Let's hope he's at the gathering, drunk."

"A gathering? The laird has much to celebrate, aye?" Adaira walked over to the hearth along the back wall.

"I hope he feasts well. It will be his last," Rafe growled.

Adaira turned and gave him a questioning look.

"'Tis not the time. Find what ye came for and let's get out of here."

"Wolves." Adaira shook her head.

Rafe followed her with the torch.

Adaira reached inside the forge. The wood was still hot, which meant the blacksmith hadn't been gone for long. She inhaled a shaky breath. *Leana needs ye.*

Carefully, she scooped a handful of ash and stood. The hairs on the back of her neck prickled as she looked toward the middle of the room. Something pulled her to that spot. She looked up at Rafe. "I need to start a fire over there." She pointed to the center of the shop.

Rafe nodded. "I'll go look for some wood."

While Rafe searched, Adaira made her way to the area. As she got closer, the air warmed around her and coiled up her body. Her skin tingled from her toes to her fingertips. Aye, there was some kind of magic here.

Rafe returned with three pieces of wood.

"Put the wood there." She pointed in front of her. "Rafe, I can already feel Leana's magic. She was here."

Rafe gave her a concerned look. "I hope we get good news."

"Aye."

Rafe placed the wood on the floor, then lit it with the torch. Adaira spread the ash she'd taken from the hearth, making a ring around the fire. "Rafe, can I have yer dirk?"

Rafe handed the weapon to her.

Adaira cut a long lock of hair off her head. She threw it in the fire and watched it curl and singe until it disappeared. She grabbed the blade and slit the palm of her right hand, then quickly held it over the flames. As soon as her blood mingled with the fire, the flames flickered angrily.

Adaira retuned the dirk, then licked the wound on her hand to make it heal. She knelt in front of the fire and closed her eyes. All fear left her body as she took in a deep breath and cleared her mind.

"I call upon the power of the blue flames. I humbly ask for the truth that lies in the past. Show me." Adaira repeated the chant three times. Her blood heated and raced through her veins. The magic was working. The sensation intensified and she opened her eyes and stared into the flames.

The fire burned blue as a scene unfolded before her. Leana danced around the Samhain fire as two men watched her with lust filled eyes. Normally this wouldn't raise concern, however Adaira couldn't shake the danger she felt lurking in the shadows. Her sister's naughty laughter echoed inside Adaira's head. She knew the laugh too well. Aye, this wasn't a good situation.

Afraid of what she'd see next, Adaira closed her eyes tight. Did she really want to know what had taken place that night? Could she live with the truth? Could she live with the fact her sister went rogue and had killed these men?

Suddenly the smell of ale mixed with burning iron struck her with concern. Knowing Leana and the alluring ways of the *Baobhan sith*, she feared the worst. Adaira opened her eyes and gasped as she flashed back in time and was standing inside the blacksmith shop cloaked by the spell. Next to the hearth she spotted the threesome tearing each other's clothes off and ravishing Leana's body. Shite, they were drowning in Leana's seduction.

Adaira took a closer look. She didn't recognize one of the men, however the lad standing behind Leana squeezing her sister's breasts was indeed Beathen.

Leana peered over Beathen's shoulder, and Adaira gasped. Her sister's eyes had turned black—a darkness Adaira knew all too well. It was the look of a *Baobhan sith* before she dragged her victim into blind passion. It was bloodlust.

Dread consumed Adaira. She couldn't believe her eyes. "Leana...nay...dinnae..." Adaira yelled into the flames.

Suddenly, black smoke rolled into the room. Confusion spread across Leana's face as the smoke engulfed them. The men didn't notice; it was as if they were under a spell. Adaira panicked. She couldn't see the men anymore, but their screams shook her to the core.

Leana covered her mouth with both hands, stifling a scream. A figure with black wings stepped from the smoke and walked toward Leana. He spread his wings, blocking Adaira's view of her sister.

"Nay!" Adaira screamed.

The fire popped. In a flash of light, the blue flame disappeared.

"Nay." Adaira frantically grabbed the wood, desperate to see more. She hissed in pain, the wood was blistering hot. She dropped it and cradled her injured hand.

Rafe kneeled next to her and took her wounded hand in his. "Adaira, are ye daft?" He pulled her shaking body against his.

"This is far more troubling than I thought," Adaira said into his chest.

"What did ye see?"

Adaira shook her head.

"Talk to me, lass." Rafe brushed her hair back from her face. "Please."

Adaira sucked in a long breath. "Leana didnae kill those lads." She picked up the ash from around the fire and smelled it. The foul stench made her stomach turn. She threw it on the ground. "The Unseelie."

"Shite," Rafe exclaimed.

"I didnae need to see his face to know who killed those men." Adaira stood, regaining her strength. "It was Alder."

Rafe's brows creased. "Alder?"

"Aye. He's one of the queen's princes. The most cunning of the three and verra powerful."

"Why didn't Leana tell ye?"

"I believe he erased the memory from her mind. When Masie found Leana, she was unconscious. Once she woke, she could no' remember anything."

"Why would he want to kill those men?"

Adaira looked up at Rafe. "Because Alder is infatuated

with Leana. He has been since she was a young lass. This was retaliation for her leaving him."

"God's bones."

"What?" Adaira questioned.

"I didn't want to believe it."

"Believe what? Tell me, Wolf."

"When Teg was out tracking Leana, he was attacked and left for dead. When he came to, he woke up in a cottage in the woods and couldn't remember how he had gotten there. All he could remember was something evil had chased him. My gut tells me the fae was involved."

"The dark prince," Adaira whispered as she looked at Rafe. "Maiden, Mother, Crone," Adaira gasped. "Teg must have been close to finding Leana."

"Who's this dark prince?"

"Alder. He's one of the queen's sons. He has always been infatuated with Leana. He's the one I saw in the spell. Rafe, he killed Cormag's son, not Leana. We need to tell the laird." Adaira began to walk to the door when Rafe stopped her.

"Hold on. Listen to yerself. A fae killed his son. He won't stand for such nonsense. No matter what the truth is, Cormag wants ye dead."

Adaira slowly turned around. "Then what are we going to do?"

"We fight and take back what is rightfully yers."

Adaira shook her head. "Cormag has nothing I want. I have made it perfectly clear. I dinnae want me father's seat as chieftain. He knows that."

"Aye, however, ye are the rightful heir. These are yer people whether ye like it or not. Cormag is power hungry, consumed by greed. He's not fit to lead. Take back what is yers."

"How? I dinnae have an army."

Rafe cupped her face and gazed into her eyes. "Ye have my pack. Heed my words, ye'll need an army to fight the fae. Win back Clan Keith and join forces with Clan Gunn. Fight the queen and win yer freedom back."

Adaira considered his words for moment. It was true, she would never be free from the laird or the queen if she did nothing. However, declaring war upon Cormag was one thing. Declaring war on the immortal Queen Snowdrop was an ambitious move. Regardless of her father's ruthless behavior, as the clan chieftain, he had been well respected. Cormag had done nothing to help the clan prosper. In ten years, her father's hard work had been destroyed, and her clan had declined into what they were now.

But would the clan fight for her?

Aye, when she'd first returned home, everyone was happy. But the rumors had spread like wildfire about how different she'd become. Could she trust her clan to fight with her?

She looked at Rafe. With him by her side, she could conquer anything.

"Wolf."

"Aye, my heart's queen."

"Do ye have the stones to fight a bastard and an evil fae queen?"

"Ye know I do." Rafe smiled and claimed her lips.

The door to the smithy shop crashed open. "Adaira Keith," a loud voice thundered. "Ye're back from the grave, lass?"

Rafe stepped in front of Adaira and unsheathed his sword, ready to gut the intruder.

Adaira peered over his shoulder. Her worst nightmare had come true. The very man who had stolen her innocence stood in the doorway, swaying back and forth. Time hadn't been kind to him. Deep, hardened lines creased his face. Gray streaked his hair.

The blacksmith staggered inside, shaking his finger at her. "Have ye come back to warm me bed?"

Rafe growled and stepped toward him.

"Nay." Adaira grabbed his arm.

"Yer father promised me land if I married ye. I did what he asked, and look where it got me." He kicked at the floor. "If it's money ye seek, I have none. The day ye left, yer father took back yer dowry and left me with nothing."

Rafe turned to Adaira. "Is this the man?"

"Aye, he's the man me father watched rape me."

"Och." The man sat down at a table. "Ye're a ghost. Ye've been dead for ten years." He hiccupped. "Wretched whore."

"I'll gut the bastard." Rafe made another move but Adaira stopped him. She walked over to the blacksmith. He was drunk and stricken with madness. In a way, she felt sorry for him, he was another one of Doughall's victims.

The smithy gazed up at her. "Be gone ghost and let me die in peace."

There was so much she wanted to say to the bastard, but didn't know where to start. "Ye will never hurt me again." Her voice wavered, but she swallowed back the tears, hating herself for allowing him to make her weak.

Her fangs lengthened. The urge to strike was at the surface waiting for her to unleash it. She wanted to kill this man, but couldn't. He couldn't hurt her ever again.

Adaira walked back to Rafe. "He's drunk and apparently has gone mad. We have what we came for. Let's leave."

Rafe grabbed her arm as she walked by. "Let me slay the devil."

"Nay. Let the bastard rot in his own hell."

Rafe growled in frustration as he approached the blacksmith.

"Rafe," Adaira called out. "Dinnae kill him."

Rafe slammed the hilt of his sword against the side of the smithy's face, knocking him out of his chair. He kicked him in the ribs, then stood over him. "Today's yer lucky day." He nudged the man's unmoving body with the toe of his boot, then spat on his face.

"Rafe!"

Rafe glared at her but didn't say a word as he followed her out of the shop. She had no words; no one had ever defended her honor like that before. As she studied her wolf's rage-filled face, Adaira knew no one would ever hurt her again, not as long as Rafe was by her side.

14

RAFE AND ADAIRA rode together on horseback through the glen. The night air helped calm his wolf, but he still wanted to go back to the smithy and kill the man who had shattered Adaira's heart when she was young.

"I don't understand why ye stopped me from gutting that bastard." Rafe finally broke the silence.

"He's gone mad. Isn't that punishment enough? Killing him would only end his suffering. Let the bastard rot."

Rafe knew she was right. Adaira was safe. He wrapped an arm around her, pulling her closer. He nuzzled her ear. "I won't apologize for hitting him with my sword."

Adaira leaned back into his embrace. "I would no' ask ye to. Thank ye for defending me honor. No one has ever done that before."

"I'll spend the rest of my life protecting ye."

"But ye have risked so much for me. I could never repay the debt."

"I could think of a way ye can start." Rafe nipped at her collarbone.

Adaira tilted her head to the side, giving him full access

to her neck. She sighed. "How could ye be thinking of such a thing at a time like this? By morn, Cormag will have his men out in full force looking for us. Ye should have taken me back to the tower."

"Let him come. There's no way I'm returning ye."

"But it would have given us more time to plan an attack."

Rafe dropped the reins and his horse continued walking down the trail. He gripped her hips. "The only thing I want to plan is me being inside ye." He kissed her neck all the way up to her earlobe. "I have everything under control. I had Teg and William set up camp deep in the woods. My pack is waiting for our arrival. It will take some time for Cormag to find. Knowing my brother, he already has a plan."

"Aye. Teg is quite resourceful."

"We have the advantage. The glen is our home, we know every trail, every stream, and every tree. We're wiser and stronger. The gods favor us. This is one battle ye don't have to fight. Trust me." He caressed her face. Something more than love and admiration shined through her gaze...trust. He'd broken through her protective barrier and left his mark on her heart.

"I love ye, Wolf," she whispered.

Gently, he rubbed his thumb across her bottom lip. She opened her mouth and sucked it in. Her tongue swirled over the tip. It took all his resolve not to take her right there. "My queen," he whispered.

He replaced his thumb with his tongue. She tasted sweeter than honey, felt softer than the finest silks, and she was his, body and soul. *Mine.*

Adaira pressed her arse against his cock. He growled. Aye, he was right where he wanted to be...under the stars with his woman. "Keep rubbing my cock with that arse and you'll pay a hefty price."

Adaira giggled. "Och, I hadn't noticed." She wiggled against him again.

Rafe nipped her shoulder as he lifted the hem of her dress up her thigh. "Ye haven't noticed?"

"Well, mayhap a wee bit."

He slid his hands along her inner thighs up betwixt her legs. "I think ye're very aware of the effect ye have on me, lass."

Adaira snaked her arm behind his neck and grabbed a handful of his hair. She pressed her body against his. "And I'm verra aware that wolves like to tease."

"Tease?" He slid his finger down her wet, hot heat as a growl of satisfaction escaped his lips. By the saints, she felt too good to be true.

"Wolf," Adaira moaned. "If this is yer way of claiming me. Then I'm yers."

Rafe paused as her words tightened in his chest. Years he'd waited for her to accept his claim, and now it was happening. He'd finally broke through her wall. "Adaira Keith," he whispered against her ear. "Ye've made me a happy man. All I have ever wanted was ye—all of ye." He

claimed her mouth with a soul shaking hunger.

"Rafe," she sighed against his lips. "I have always been yers. I was too stubborn to admit it."

"Aye, stubborn as a mule."

"Och," Adaira exclaimed and elbowed him in the ribs. "I'm no' that stubborn."

"Damn, woman," he gasped from the blow. "Ye know I wouldn't have ye any other way." He brushed her hair away from her neck. "I love yer rough edges." He trailed soft kisses from the nape of her neck, right below her ear, down to her shoulder.

She shivered, causing him to grin like the devil. "Shall I continue, my queen?" He ran his finger down her womanhood, touching her deep inside.

"Aye," she moaned. "Dinnae ever stop touching me."

God's bones, this woman drove him daft with passion. He was hers to command. Masterfully, he stroked her faster until her legs began to quiver.

She threw her head back. "By the saints, Rafe," she moaned. He kissed her neck as she rested her head against his chest.

His name coming from her lips drove his inner beast wild. Rafe reached around Adaira and untied the top of her dress. He cupped her breasts, wishing they could stop so he could claim her properly. He wanted her nipples in his mouth. He wanted to hear her moan his name again and again. Shite, he had to find a place to stop.

Horses thundered through the glen. Rafe paused. Someone was coming their way. He pulled the top of Adaira's dress up, then reached for his claymore. He sniffed the air. "Shite."

"What's wrong," she asked.

"Teg and William. They are riding toward us."

Adaira studied the path ahead of them. "I dinnae see them."

"Keep looking. They'll be here." Rafe grabbed the reins.

"Yer senses are incredible, Wolf," Adaira said.

"I'm in my element out here." He kissed the back of her head. "Don't think for one minute that I'm done with ye, my queen. When we get to camp, ye're mine."

"Dinnae make promises ye can no' keep," Adaira teased.

Rafe growled as his brother approached.

"Brother," Teg greeted too eagerly. "It took ye long enough."

"We had an unexpected visitor," Adaira said.

"An unexpected visitor?" Teg questioned.

"Nothing to fret over," Rafe said. "Has camp been set up?"

"Aye." Teg answered. "The pack is ready for yer command."

Rafe nodded as he followed Teg back to camp.

The garrison was spread out and hidden within the glen. The soldiers were preparing their weapons for battle. He observed a group of young men sitting around a fire, grimly staring into the flames. Battle was on their minds.

Rafe dismounted, then helped Adaira down from the horse. "Teg, take Adaira to my tent and make sure she's cared for, then meet William and I back here to go over our strategy."

Teg nodded.

Before Adaira was escorted away, Rafe kissed the top of her head. "I'll join ye shortly, my queen."

Adaira cupped his face. "Be brave and bold, Wolf."

"'Tis all I know how to be." He dipped his head down and claimed her lips.

Adaira broke the kiss. "Dinnae make me wait long." She winked, then followed Teg to the tent.

Rafe couldn't shake the grim faces of those young men he'd seen as he approached camp from his mind. He remembered his first battle and knew what was running through these lad's minds. *Will I live to see another day? Will I see my pack again?*

Rafe began to make his way to the men when his squire approached.

"Master Rafe," the lad bowed. "Make I take yer horse?"

Rafe handed him the reins. "Take good care of her." He patted the mare on the hind quarters.

"Aye," the lad replied.

The lads stood and bowed as their Alpha approached.

"Please rise," Rafe said.

The group stood at attention.

"The eve of battle can play on a man's mind. But know this, we are wolves. Our forefathers were warriors. It's in our blood to stand and fight".

The lads looked at each other.

"Have faith in yer wolf and yer forefathers. The warrior is in ye."

"Master Rafe." One of the men stepped forward.

"Aye."

"I won't let ye down. I'll proudly die for my Alpha."

One-by-one, each warrior stepped forward and knelt in front of Rafe. Their lives were in his hands. They fought for him. Words couldn't describe what he was feeling. "Yer loyalty won't be forgotten." Rafe clasped one of the men on the shoulder as he made his way to join Teg and William with tomorrows battle heavy on his own mind.

As he approached, he heard William and Teg arguing inside William's tent. Before entering, Rafe took in a long breath. *They shouldn't be wasting time arguing on the eve of battle.* Rafe stepped inside and the men grew quiet.

A map of the area surrounding Castle Dornoch was open on the ground. Miniature wolf heads and armored knights were arranged on the map.

"Brother, do we have a plan of attack?" Teg asked.

"I propose we storm the castle. Hit them in the ballocks," William offered.

Teg shook his head. "Our numbers are too small. It will never work."

"Then what's yer suggestion? Tuck our tails and run?" William spat.

The two men bantered until Rafe couldn't take it anymore. "Enough," he exclaimed. "We'll get slaughtered if we stand divided. Do ye understand me?"

"Aye," the men said in unison.

Rafe paced, stopping to look at the map occasionally. "We don't have time to build traps, nor the numbers to storm the castle."

"We can outwit the bastards," Teg said.

Rafe divided the wolf pieces into two groups. One placed in the glen, the other heading toward Dornoch. "We'll attack them at home and on the battlefield." He studied the wolf pieces.

"That's madness," Teg exclaimed.

"Nay, young pup. That's having the ballocks to stand up and fight," William said.

Rafe continued. "Cormag will send his troops our way, leaving the castle lightly guarded." He pointed to the glen. "One group will stay hidden here. The other will ride back to Dornoch." Rafe slid a knight piece into the glen. "They'll be looking for our camp. What they don't know, is our wolves will be hunting them. I'll cut them off before they reach camp."

Rafe looked at Teg, then to William. He saw the wolf in each of their eyes.

"Teg, ye'll lead the men on horseback."

"Aye."

"William, command the infantry."

"Aye."

"We'll use the glen to our advantage. We know these bastards have no experience out here. But we do," Rafe said as he clasped William's shoulder.

A sly grin spread across William's face. "My Alpha." He nodded and left.

Rafe looked over at Teg. "What is it?"

"This is an ambitious plan."

"Aye, but if we want our freedom from Cormag, we must fight for it. I understand if ye've changed yer mind."

"Nay, Brother. Ye have my sword."

"Good." Rafe exhaled. "I need ye to do something for me."

"Anything."

"I want ye to take Adaira with you back to Dornoch."

"Wouldn't she be safer here, with ye?" Teg looked confused.

"Nay. Cormag will be dead by the time ye reach Dornoch. Yer men can fight off what resistance remains."

"As ye wish."

Rafe had to convince Adaira to leave without him. He needed her safe so he could fight without worrying about her. It was going to be a bloody battle. "I'll see to it that Adaira is ready. At dawn, I want ye, yer men, and Adaira out of here."

"Aye." Teg began to walk out but stopped. "Brother, may I ask where ye'll be?"

Rage settled over him. "I'm going to remind Cormag who the true leader of the clan is...then I'm going to kill him." For Adaira first, and then for his pack. Honor must be restored at all costs.

15

"Nay, I will no' leave ye to fight Cormag alone." Adaira couldn't believe what she was hearing.

"Adaira, I'm not asking ye, I'm telling ye. Ye will leave tomorrow with Teg and go back to Dornoch and wait for my return."

"How could ye make me do such a thing?" She folded her arms over her chest. "This is *our* fight, Wolf."

Rafe grabbed her shoulders. "'Tis the safest place for ye to be."

Adaira yanked free. "I'm no' a treasure ye keep locked away because ye're scared I'll break. I have the strength to fight."

"And I don't question that. This battle is different. These are troubled times, and desperate men will do desperate things to survive. I cannot have ye on the battlefield worried that Cormag has gotten to ye."

Adaira rubbed the chill from her arms. The thought of leaving him made her feel empty inside. She'd failed in protecting Leana. She couldn't fail Rafe, too. "If I leave, who'll protect ye?"

Rafe placed his finger under her chin, tipping it up. "My heart's queen, I need ye to be somewhere safe."

"I want to be here with ye. I'd never forgive meself if something happened to you—"

"I don't plan on dying any time soon."

Adaira looked deep into his eyes and she knew there was nothing she could say or do to change his mind. "Stubborn wolf."

"Stubborn lass." He grinned. "Promise me ye'll leave with Teg."

Adaira looked away.

"Adaira," he warned.

Goddess, she loved the deep tone of his voice.

"Don't make me bend ye over my knee, lass."

She looked up at him with a seductive smile.

A growl escaped his lips. He wrapped his arm around her waist and pulled her close. Hunger brewed behind his smoldering gaze.

She cupped the back of his neck and brought his mouth to hers. She teased his top lip with a flick of her tongue, Rafe pulled away, taking a step back. "God's bones, woman. I'm hanging on by a thread. Promise me."

She needed Rafe's hands on her body like the air she breathed. "I promise."

Before she could mutter another word, Rafe claimed her lips. He grabbed her arse with both hands and lifted her up. She locked her ankles behind his back and her arms around his neck as Rafe made his way to the pallet in the corner of the tent.

She tore his tunic off as he laid her down on the furs. She ran her hands down his muscled chest to his plaid. She unwrapped the material slowly, until his manhood sprang free.

He gazed down her body. "Ye set me on fire, lass." Adaira rolled over so she was on top of him. She caressed his stubbled cheek as she smiled. Rafe had taught her how to love. For the first time, she allowed Rafe to see her in the flesh with nothing to hide. She wasn't holding back. She leaned forward, resting her forehead against his. "I love ye, Wolf."

"And I, ye." He plunged his hands through her hair and stared into her eyes as if he saw straight through to her soul. "One day, very soon, we'll be able to love freely. No more hiding."

"Aye." She smiled.

She brushed her lips over his, trailing kisses across his cheek, chin, and down his neck, savoring the spicy taste of his skin. Tonight she was going to devour every inch of him. If she had to go back to Dornoch without Rafe, she'd make damned sure she'd be in his dreams.

She moved down his body. He moaned as she licked his nipples.

She nipped and kissed her way to his muscled stomach, scratching her nails down his chest at the same time. Desire burned within her as she thought about giving him the same pleasure as he'd given her before. She gazed up at him —his eyes were beautiful. Everything about him made her feel like a woman. "I want ye," she said.

"Adaira Keith, ye tease me daft."

Seductively, she snaked up his body. "I assure ye, me love, I am no tease." He let out a hiss of pleasure as she wrapped her hand around his cock and stroked him.

"I need ye to promise me something," Adaira whispered against his ear.

"Anything ye want, my queen."

"When I'm gone, dream of me."

He brushed her cheek with the back of his hand. "Always."

16

THE NEXT MORNING, while Rafe waited for Adaira to wake up, he saddled a horse for her. Usually his squire would do it, but Rafe had to keep his mind busy. With every minute that passed, Adaira was closer to leaving. Holding firm to his choice was going to be tough. He'd fought the urge to run inside the tent and make love to his queen again. It was a distraction he didn't need. The sooner Adaira left, the sooner he could execute his plan to kill Cormag.

"Ye dinnae come back to bed." Adaira stood on the other side of the horse running her hand through the gray mare's mane.

"I didn't want to wake ye."

Silence fell between them, her pending departure hanging over them like a dark cloud.

Teg finally joined them. "'Tis time to go."

"Aye," Rafe agreed, though he wanted Adaira to stay. He walked to Adaira and lifted her hands to his mouth, kissing each one.

"Dinnae tell me goodbye."

Rafe wiped a tear from her cheek. "I love ye, Adaira Keith."

Adaira frowned, reminding him of a wee girl.

Rafe chuckled.

"What's so funny?" she asked.

"All this time, I fought to make ye love me. And now that ye're mine, I have to let ye go."

"Rafe." Her voice wavered as she shook her head. "Please, let me stay."

"Ye know I cannot allow it. Teg will keep ye safe until I return."

He cupped her cheek. His heart was being torn from his chest. "Look at me." She did, her pretty eyes filled with tears. "Tell me ye love me."

Adaira wrapped her arms around his neck. He pulled her close, marveling at the softness of her body. "Wolf," she whispered in his ear, a sound he'd never forget. "Come back to me." He felt her breath seize in her chest. "I love ye."

He nuzzled her neck, taking in her sweet scent. He would never forget her love, for it was his singular reason to fight.

"My lady," Teg said as he halted his horse next to them. "We must leave."

"Aye," Adaira said as Rafe lifted her into the saddle.

She met Rafe's gaze a last time, then focused straight ahead. He knew it was her way of showing him that she was strong enough to handle whatever the future held. He patted the mare on the arse. "Godspeed."

Teg and Adaira, followed by fifty men, rode out of the camp.

William joined Rafe. "She'll make a good chieftain."

Rafe nodded. "Aye. Our plan must work."

"We're all behind ye, my lord.."

Rafe looked around. The Honor Guard, five hundred strong, surrounded him, ready for battle. They didn't have weapons or armor; their way of fighting resided in their blood. A wolf who was standing in the middle of the pack howled, and the rest followed. The thrill of the shift was in the air. Rafe's beast came alive and he watched, as one by one, his pack shift into their wolves.

The wolves broke away into small groups, running into the glen with a solid plan, to isolate the enemy—to seek out the weakest and attack. They didn't need a commander. These wolves knew what to do.

William shifted into a black wolf.

With the scent of the shift in the air, Rafe felt the earth's savage pulse. The hair on the back of his neck stood up. His vision narrowed to shades of red. Wildness raced through his veins as he sought out the wolf inside him.

In his silver and black wolf form, Rafe ran deep into the glen. No matter how many times he shifted, he'd never tire of the feeling of being free and connected to the land.

Rafe came to a halt as he caught up with his pack. He paused and sniffed the air. *Cormag.* He snarled. A cold wind blew through his fur, sending a chill down his spine. The hunt was on.

Rafe ran deeper into the woods, following Cormag's trail and the sound of thundering hooves rushing through the glen. The scent grew stronger. The bastard was so close he could hear their teeth chattering from the cold. Aye, Cormag and his men were near.

Throughout the night the Honor Guard herded Clan Keith like sheep and stalked them right into Rafe's trap. The entourage was exhausted and now lost.

To Rafe's advantage, Cormag had no idea he'd been stalked for miles and had been thrown off track. It wouldn't be long until the Mad Dog surfaced and ripped through the bastard's flesh. The laird motioned for his men to halt. This was right where Rafe wanted him.

"My laird," Hamish, one of Cormag's men called out. "I believe we've been here before."

"Aye, we've been riding in circles with no sign of those traitorous wolves," Cormag said.

"It will be dark soon. We should make camp," Hamish advised.

"Aye, but do no' let yer guard down," Cormag warned. "The bloody bastards are out there. I can feel their eyes upon us."

As it grew darker, the cold wind picked up, but it had no effect on the wolves as they watched their enemy from the shadows. In this unforgiving terrain, it didn't take much to wear down a mortal man. The wolves used this to their advantage, too.

As the last of the men retired, the wolves snuck into camp.

The first group slaughtered the guards on watch. Before the men could scream, their necks were snapped, their flesh ripped from their bones. Then the rest wolves stormed the tents.

In the still of the night, Cormag's men shot out of their tents bloodied and screaming in terror as they ran for their lives. The brave warriors who thought they could best a wolf stayed behind, giving it their best effort to survive. However, their swords were no match for the wolves sharp teeth and their powerful strength. The surprise attack was swift and brutal.

The stench of blood filled the air causing Rafe's mouth to water like a salivating dog. He could taste Cormag's blood. It was time.

He knew exactly were Cormag slept. He crept closer to the tent, then paused as he saw Cormag step outside with his sword in hand. His men were being dragged out of their tents and torn limb-from-limb.

"Kill every wolf in sight," the laird called.

That's when the Mad Dog unleashed and Rafe charged the laird. Cormag turned around—his eyes widened in fear as Rafe lunged through the air, knocking him to the ground. The force of the fall sent them both tumbling in a heap of fur and flesh. Rafe rolled off the laird and stood. As he shook free from the fall, he noticed Cormag clawing through the snow to his dropped sword.

Rafe catapulted in the laird's direction, clamping his teeth down on his arse. Cormag screamed and rolled over, kicking his feet. "Traitor!"

Rafe growled and circled Cormag, stopping inches from his throat. He snapped his teeth, scaring the man so bad he begged for God's mercy. Rafe howled before he made his final move. He tore viciously and mercilessly at Cormag's neck, the taste of blood igniting the savagery inside him.

He'd kill the bastard slowly.

Cormag hit Rafe in the head with the hilt of his sword. Rafe yelped in pain and lost his grip on Cormag's throat.

The laird staggered to his feet, holding his bloody neck. "Ye think ye can defeat me, wolf?" He pointed his sword at Rafe. Blood dripped from the blade. "Both of us will no' see another day." Cormag breathed heavily. "But I will be victorious."

Rafe growled. Cormag couldn't be more wrong—Rafe had everything to live for. He edged toward the laird, motivated by rage and hatred. Without hesitation, he charged. A sharp pain shot through his hind leg and Rafe fell to the ground. He whimpered, then smelled his own blood. He didn't know what was happening. He looked behind him—a trail of crimson soaked the snow. Blood was seeping from his hind leg. He hadn't felt Cormag's sword pierce his body...until now.

With all the strength he had left, Rafe forced his injured body up. Before he could regain his balance, Cormag charged him. With only three legs to stand on, and pain shooting through his body, Rafe couldn't move out of the way fast enough. The laird stabbed Rafe in the gut.

Rafe howled as both of them hit the ground.

17

"My lady. We must go. No more stalling," Teg called from over his shoulder as he gave Adaira her privacy from the other side of the tree.

Adaira had pretended she needed to relieve herself, this being the third stop during their short journey away from the camp. Aye, she was stalling, trying to find any reason to get back to Rafe. She'd given it her best effort, but she couldn't leave her love behind—not when he was fighting for her freedom and right as the true leader of her clan. Something warned her Rafe needed her.

"Rafe will be furious if we don't get ye back to Dornoch."

"Aye, I suppose he will...if he makes it back alive, "Adaira said.

"He'll make it," Teg snapped. "Have ye lost faith in him?"

"Nay. It's just I can no' stand back and do nothing while he risks his life for me. I need to be there with him."

"Ye love him?"

Aye, her heart skipped a beat when she heard his name. Her stomach fluttered when he touched her. She lost her breath when he kissed her. Aye, she would die if it meant he'd live.

"Well, do ye?" Teg pressed.

"I do."

"Then do me a favor."

"Aye."

"Do as ye're told and no one will get hurt."

She emerged from behind the tree and placed her hands on her hips. "Ye're as stubborn as yer brother."

Teg turned around. "It runs in the family."

A yelp echoed through the forest. Their eyes met, wide and stunned. Her heart raced with fear. "Rafe," Adaira whispered.

Teg nodded. That nagging sensation she'd been feeling became harsh reality. Rafe needed her, them.

Like a flash of lightning, Adaira ran through the forest, back to Rafe. She could hear Teg in wolf form right behind her. As she leapt over fallen trees, she prayed that Rafe was alive. It wasn't long before she reached a camp site. Her heart sank to her stomach as she watched Cormag standing over Rafe. He pulled his sword from Rafe's gut.

"Nay," Adaira cried out. She gripped her stomach, feeling the blade as it had left Rafe's body.

Cormag looked up, and their gazes locked. Stumbling toward her with a victorious grin on his face, he said, "Ye're are next, wench. Today the Keith curse will be broken."

Her eyes darkened. Rage boiled inside her body unlike anything she'd ever felt before. Something dark unleashed inside her...an evil she could no longer contain. She stretched her arms out and long, black nails extended out of her fingertips. She let out a hiss, exposing her dagger-like fangs.

Cormag dropped his sword, stunned by her changed

appearance. Adaira reached him in two steps, grabbing him by the throat. "I am no curse, Cormag. My sister didnae kill yer son. And if I told ye the truth about who did, ye still would no' believe me. Yer bent on vengeance." Adaira lifted him off the ground like he weighed no more than a helpless child.

Something stopped her though—an echo from the past, a memory of the girl she used to be. She'd never been so angry before, never wanted to kill so desperately. She thirsted for blood, not the kind to keep her alive, but blood-vengeance, the very thing Cormag was guilty of. A shiver streaked down her spine. This wasn't really what she had become, was it?

Rafe whimpered, drawing her attention away from Cormag. She let go of the laird and looked over at her wolf. Rafe was lying in a pool of his own blood, dying.

"Rafe!" Adaira rushed to him. "Wolf." She fell to her knees. She didn't know what to do. How was she going to save him?

She leaned over Rafe to listen to his heartbeat when a sharp pain struck her back and shot through to her stomach. She bent over in pain, something was protruding out of her skin. "What the..." She looked down, the end of a sword was sticking out of her gut.

Slowly, Adaira stood and turned around.

Cormag could hardly keep his balance. "Ye should never turn yer back on yer enemy."

Adaira reached behind her and grabbed the hilt of the sword. Slowly, she pulled the blade out of her. "And ye should no' have taken me kindness for granted."

Terror streaked across his face as he watched the gaping hole in Adaira's stomach heal.

"No blade can kill me, eegit."

Cormag back stepped, shocked at what he'd witnessed. "Nay!"

Her vision turned red. *Maiden, Mother, Crone, forgive me,* she prayed as she lifted the sword. In one fluid motion, she threw the blade directly into Cormag's chest.

Fury erupted inside her like nothing she'd ever felt before. How dare this man try to kill her wolf? Suddenly, the leash she'd been tethered to snapped and she charged Cormag. As he saw her running toward him, he raised his hands in surrender. But it was too late. There was no stopping the wrath of a blood drinker. She clawed at him mercilessly, reliving all her pain and sorrow, finally finding a worthy recipient for her pent-up rage.

Adaira kicked him in the stomach, sending him to the ground. Deep slashes covered his body and were bleeding out quickly. Though Adaira needed to feed, the thought of drinking Cormag's blood turned her stomach.

She knelt beside him. "Ye were right. The curse plaguing me clan will end today," she whispered in his ear, "Say hello to Beathen." She snapped his neck, ending the threat to her family.

Adaira sat back on her heels, staring at Cormag. It was done, and she would never regret her choice.

"Adaira," Teg called out.

She stood and ran over to Teg, who was in human form, kneeling beside his brother.

"He's badly wounded and cannot shift," Teg said.

Adaira fell to her knees. Blood poured from Rafe's stomach wound. "Wolf, I'm here." She ran her fingers through his fur. "Do no' leave me." She swallowed back the tears. "Teg, what are we going to do? I dinnae know how to save a wolf."

"Let's get him inside a tent and warm him up."

Adaira nodded. She helped carry Rafe to the nearest shelter. They laid him on a pallet.

William joined them. "Shite," he exclaimed, looking at his fallen Alpha.

"The wound is deep. And there's another on his hind leg," Teg said as he examined his brother's body. "He's lost a lot of blood."

"Aye," William agreed.

"I can give him mine," Adaira said as she shouldered her way between the two men.

"Ye have done enough." Teg glared at her.

"Teg, this is no' me fault. I begged him to let me stay and help fight."

"Are ye that self-righteous that ye actually believe that if ye had stayed and fought, Rafe wouldn't be wounded? I swear, Adaira, if Rafe dies..." Teg choked back the tears.

"Tegwyn," William warned. "We all agreed to fight. I know ye want to place blame on someone, but this is no' her fault."

Teg shook his head, his disappointment and anger clear.

"Me blood can heal humans. Can it help a wolf?" Adaira asked.

William scratched his chin. "I don't know. It's risky."

"What do ye mean? Me blood can fight infection."

"Aye, lass. That is the problem. Rafe is a wolf. Yer blood will kill his wolf."

Adaira's heart plummeted. Her blood could kill him? "Are ye sure?"

"I have not witnessed it myself, but the rumors are enough to tread softly. No wolf will risk losing their kindred spirit."

"So, there's hope," Adaira said. "No one knows for certain whether a *Baobhan sith's* blood will kill a wolf?"

"Aye," William confirmed.

"Ye'll stay away from him." Tegwyn pointed at Adaira. "As his brother, I know him better than any of ye. He'd die before he'd risk killing his wolf."

"Teg, if we do nothing, he'll die anyway. Please, let me try to help him," Adaira begged. "I can no' lose him."

Teg looked to William. Adaira prayed they would allow her to help, because nothing was going to stop her from saving the man she loved.

Finally, William nodded.

"Rafe would never accept losing his wolf," Teg said grimly. "He'd want to die like a warrior, he deserves that respect."

"I understand, Tegwyn," Adaira said, tears burning her eyes. "B-but I canna lose him."

Teg stepped away from the pallet and looked at Adaira. There was deep sadness in his eyes. Had he changed his mind, then? Would he let her save the man she loved?

"Save him, *all of him*." Teg left the tent.

Before departing, William placed his hand on her shoulder. "I have faith in ye, lass. Bring him home."

Quickly, Adaira knelt beside Rafe. His breathing was labored, he was in a lot of pain. She examined the wound on his stomach, it was fatal. She bit into her wrist, then held it over the wound, letting drops of her blood fall on it. Her wolf whimpered. This was a good sign that her blood was already doing its job. She caressed his head. "Shhh, my love. Today is no' yer day to fade into the void."

Within moments, his skin started to stitch back together and his breathing slowed down. Because he was too weak to shift back into his human form, he couldn't drink her blood. Adaira held her wrist over Rafe's mouth and drops of blood fell on his tongue. "Drink, Wolf." He didn't move. "Drink," she demanded. "Ye have to drink."

He didn't move.

What was happening? "Nay, Rafe." Panicked, she felt for a pulse. It was weak and erratic. "Nay," she sobbed. "Ye can no' leave me, Wolf. Do ye hear me? Ye can no' leave me."

She cradled his head on her lap and rocked back and forth. "I'm so sorry. I failed to protect ye, just like my sisters." Anger surfaced inside her as she contemplated a future they would never share. "This is no' fair. We were so close to being happy."

No matter how close she came to happiness, she'd never reach it. It wasn't her fate. "I love ye, Wolf."

She sobbed through the night, blaming herself for his impending death. *He'd still be alive if it was no' for me.* She curled up next to Rafe, snuggled against his fur. She took in her wolf's spicy scent which only made her break down more. This couldn't be the last time she'd hold her wolf, feel his warmth, or touch his soft fur. She closed her tear-filled eyes. He had to live.

The night had been long and worrisome for Adaira as she laid by her wolf; never leaving his side. Heavy footsteps paced outside the tent alerted her morn was here. Rafe's pack were waiting for news about the condition of their Alpha. However, Adaira didn't want to open her eyes and face the fact that her wolf could be dead. As long as she felt him next to her, she could go on believing he was alive.

Nay. They deserved to know. She had to know.

Praying to the gods for a miracle, she opened her eyes. Stunned to meet Rafe's gaze, she stared deep into his gaze. He'd survived the night? By the gods...Was this fae trickery?

"I've always loved watching ye sleep." Rafe brushed her hair back from her face.

Adaira touched his face. "Is this a dream?"

"Nay, I'm here."

Her heart felt like it was going to burst with joy. She wrapped her arms around him. "I thought ye were dead."

"Just resting," he teased.

"Dinnae ever scare me like that again." She blinked, shocked and pleased his body had healed—even more grateful that his sense of humor was intact. "How are ye feeling, Wolf? Do ye need more blood?"

"Blood?"

"Aye, I gave ye me blood to heal ye."

Rafe sat up, shoving his hands through his hair. "Do ye know what ye have done?"

"Aye, Teg told me about the risks." Adaira's brows creased. "Rafe, are ye mad at me?" She watched his jaw tighten. "I saved yer life."

"'Tis not much of a life without my wolf."

"We dinnae know that ye lost yer wolf. Ye need time to fully heal. I can help." She stood, looking down at him.

"I think ye should go."

Was he really throwing her out after everything they'd been through? How could he blame her for saving him? "Fine, I'll go. Ye'll need someone to set yer leg. Should I send Teg in?"

"Do as ye will." He wouldn't look at her. He stared at the ceiling as a tear rolled down his cheek. She wanted to comfort him, but it was perfectly clear he needed time to think, and she was the last person he wanted to confide in.

Adaira left the tent, holding back the tears. She knew she could never replace the love he had for his wolf. But wasn't she worth living for?

Teg was sitting by the fire. He slowly stood and wiped his hands down his plaid as she approached. "Is he—"

"Alive? Aye."

Teg sighed with relief.

"However, he's angry."

"His wolf?"

"Aye."

Teg shook his head. "I knew it. This isn't going to sit well with him."

"But he's alive. He just needs time to heal."

"Can I see him?"

"Aye. Rafe still needs his leg set. He will no' allow me to help."

"I'll take care of it."

"As soon as he's able to ride, we're leaving for Dornoch," Adaira commanded. "Now that the battle is over, I need to find Leana."

Teg nodded. "I've already sent word back to Dornoch that Laird Cormag is dead. His head on a spike should be enough proof."

"Thank ye." She walked away.

18

MASIE LOOKED DOWN and rubbed her stomach. "Are ye sure, Ina?"

"Aye. Ye are with child."

Masie's heart swelled with happiness. "I can no' believe it." She giggled. "Kerr and I are having a wee one."

The disappointment on Ina's face didn't go unnoticed. Dread crept over Masie as her past with Ina surfaced. It hadn't been easy for her to forgive Ina for placing a spell on her and trying to turn Kerr against her all because of the witch's love for Masie's husband. However, in Massie's time of need, Ina had a change of heart and helped her fight back against the fae queen's magic that left Masie weak. For that, she was grateful.

Their friendship had grown over the months. They'd even found something in common, witchcraft. Masie had always been intrigued with spells, but never had anyone to teach her. When Masie asked Ina to show her, Ina was pleased to do so.

"I'm sure Kerr will be happy about the news." Ina walked over to the water basin and washed her hands.

As much as Ina was trying to hide her displeasure, Masie saw right through her. "Ina, I can tell this news does no' sit well with ye."

Ina wiped her hands dry on a cloth. "I'm fine."

Ina turned around and Masie met her gaze. "I dinnae believe ye. I know how much ye love Kerr. I need ye to be honest with me."

Ina exhaled.

"Please. Ye can no' tell me the child I'm carrying does no' change our relationship. Ina, I enjoy yer company. But if ye can no' be honest with me and tell me how ye're feeling, I can no longer trust ye."

"Masie." Ina walked over to the bed where Masie was resting and sat down. "Ye're right. The news of yer child is like a dagger through my heart. There will always be a part of me that loves Kerr, but our friendship is more important."

"Aye. I never thought we'd become friends."

"I was a nasty witch to ye."

They giggled.

"I'm glad ye're a witch. I would no' have survived the queen's spell without ye."

Ina cleared her throat. "Ye want to know the sex of yer babe?"

Masie's eyes widened. "Ye can do that? I'm barely showing."

Ina stood and walked over to the dresser, pulling the top drawer out. "Aye. 'Tis auld magic, but my stone has never been wrong." Ina pulled a gray stone out of a small, leather bag.

"A stone is going to tell me boy or girl?"

Ina returned to Masie. "This is no' any auld stone. This stone has been passed down through my family for generations. With each pregnancy, a fertility spell was placed upon the stone. It was used to help women conceive and tell the sex of their babes. With each baby born, the power of the stone has become stronger."

Masie listened intently.

Ina placed the stone on Masie's navel. A warm sensation tingled through her body, then the stone glowed. "What's happening?" Masie gazed at the stone, then Ina—worried.

"Shhh. Do no' move."

Masie swallowed her fear, knowing she should trust her friend.

A moment later, Ina picked up the stone. She closed her eyes, chanting words Masie didn't understand. After what seemed like forever, Ina finally presented the stone to her.

"Ina, what does this mean?"

Ina opened her eyes and looked at the stone. She gasped.

Masie sat up. "What is it?"

"I've never seen anything like it."

"Please, tell me what's going on."

"The stone will glow the color of one of the parents' eyes which indicates boy or girl."

Masie looked at the stone and squealed, "It's a boy. The stone is green."

"Aye, but wait. Look deeper into the stone."

Masie took the stone from Ina. She looked deeper. "There's a darkness swirling in the middle. What does this mean? Is there something wrong with the babe?"

"Nay, he's a blood drinker."

All the joy and happiness surrounding Masie's heart faded. *A blood drinker?*

"Masie," Ina held her hand. "This babe could cause ye much harm. He'll be ravenous and drain ye of life. Ye must be watched verra closely."

Masie placed her hand on her stomach. "I dinnae want it." A tear rolled down her face.

"Ye must no' think that way. This babe was meant to be." Ina smiled. "Once ye tell Kerr, ye'll change yer mind."

Masie stood and adjusted her dress. How was she going to tell Kerr? He would never accept the monster inside her? "Nay, I will no' tell him."

"Ye have to tell him. Ye're his wife."

"Nay. Dinnae ye have a spell to take care of this?"

Ina hugged her.

"I can no' have this babe," Masie cried.

"Shhh." Ina tried to console her.

A knock at the door startled Masie. "Masie, lass, are ye in there?" Kerr called.

Masie looked at Ina, scared to death. "I can no' tell him."

"Ye must." Ina swiped the tears from Masie's face. "Trust in him."

"Masie," Kerr exclaimed.

"Aye, love." She cleared her throat and brushed the rest of the tears away.

Kerr opened the door. "I bring ye good news this morn, my angel." He kissed her cheek, then greeted Ina.

"Good morn, Commander Kerr." Ina bowed. "I was just leaving."

Kerr nodded as Ina left the bedchamber.

"What good news do ye bring?" Masie asked.

"I have word that Laird Keith has fallen in battle."

"What?"

"Aye, Adaira is now the chieftain. The Gunn and Keith feud is over."

Masie wrapped her arms around Kerr. "I can no' believe it."

"Adaira would like to see ye. We'll leave in the morn."

Masie stepped out of his embrace, her gaze averted.

"I thought ye'd be happy to see yer sister." Kerr tipped her chin up so she had to look at him. "We dinnae have to go."

Tears rolled down her face. "I do want to go."

"What's wrong."

"Nothing." She walked to the window and looked out as she gathered her strength.

"Those are no' happy tears, Masie." He walked up behind her and wrapped his arms around her waist. "Tell me what ails ye and I'll slay it," he teased.

Masie knew the truth behind his words. He'd kill anything that dared harm her.

"Ye can no' slay this problem, me love." She placed her hand on her stomach. "I'm with child."

Silence sliced through the room. He was emotionless as she waited nervously for his response. Was he thinking what she had failed to—how was this going to work? The silence was driving her daft. "Kerr, say something." She turned to face him.

Kerr shoved his hands through his hair and began to pace. "A wee one?"

Masie nodded. "I understand if ye dinnae want it. This pregnancy happened too fast, before we had a chance to talk about children." Masie looked to the floor, rubbing her hands together. "Ina says it's a boy."

Kerr gave pause. "A boy."

Masie closed her eyes, afraid to see the disappointment in his eyes when she told him the babe's true nature. "He's a blood drinker."

She heard his heart skip a beat. She opened her eyes and watched Kerr's face harden as he took in the news.

"Please... I will no' keep him if it means losing ye. In fact, I dinnae know if I want him."

"Masie," Kerr whispered.

"Nay. I've cursed our son." Tears streamed down her face.

Kerr took her in his arms and kissed the top of her head. "Ye didnae curse our son, love. He's got the best of us inside him." She looked up and Kerr cupped her face. "This is our bairn. I will no' turn me back on our child, no matter what. I'm proud to be yer husband and now the father of yer children. We'll get through this, together."

Masie nodded.

Kerr placed his hands on her stomach. "A son?"

Masie looked down at Kerr's hands as he rubbed her stomach. Happiness, unlike anything she'd ever felt before, swelled in her chest. They were going to have a wee one. "Aye."

19

THE SWEET SMELL of honey woke Rafe from a deep sleep. He knew who had been in his bedchamber. Every night since they'd returned to Dornoch, Adaira left provisions on the table next to his bed.

Rafe winced as he rolled over onto his back and looked around the room in hope of catching a glimpse of Adaira, but she'd already left. She hadn't said a word to him since their fight, nor did he want her to. He was still angry. Angry that she didn't listen to him and stay away from the battle. Angry that he couldn't use his right leg. Angry that her blood killed his wolf. How could she do this to him? It was a warrior's right to die in battle with honor. Now he was nothing more than a broken-down man.

He eyed the wound on his gut. It was healed but still tender. His leg injury had left him a cripple, dependent on the walking stick propped next to the bed. The damned thing humiliated him, reminding him of his weakness. He'd rather die than fall on his arse one more time. He didn't need a crutch. He needed his wolf.

"I see ye're still pouting like a child."

Rafe closed his eyes, irritated by his brother who was sitting at his bedside. "Who let ye in? Did Adaira send ye?"

"Nay, I don't need an invitation," Teg said. "'Tis time somebody came in here and kicked yer arse."

Rafe laughed. "And here I thought ye were here to entertain me."

"This is no joke," Teg huffed. "Stop feeling sorry for yerself and get out of bed."

Rafe glared at his brother. "I wouldn't be in this predicament if ye and Adaira hadn't taken it upon yerselves to interfere with my fate."

Teg stood. "Ye were dying. We did what any normal person with a heart would do."

"Yer heart has left me a cripple. What good is a warrior without his leg or wolf? Answer me, Teg. Then I might consider getting out of bed."

"Do ye think it was easy for me to make the decision? Ye're still our Alpha, the pack needs ye. Adaira needs ye. Besides, ye still have yer other leg."

Rafe didn't respond. Though he was furious, the sound of Adaira's name still made his heart jump. How was he going to help her fight the queen when he wasn't whole? Furthermore, the pack wouldn't stand behind a weak leader. Nay, it was time to step aside.

"I know what ye're thinking, Brother," Teg said. "Ye're wrong. Where's yer will to fight? Where's the man who never breaks a promise? Ye promised Adaira ye'd help her fight the fae queen and find her sister."

Rafe sat up. "Do ye know how it feels to lose yer wolf?"

Teg shook his head.

"'Tis like there's a hole in my heart, an empty pit that I cannot fill. Not even Adaira's love can fill it." He placed his hand over his chest, "I mourn for something I cannot have. I know I've made promises and it tears me up knowing I cannot fulfill them."

"Have ye tried to call forth yer wolf?"

"Need ye even ask?"

"Mayhap, ye need more time to heal."

"Teg, I don't have time. The pack needs a strong leader." Rafe reached over to the table next to the bed and picked up a brooch. He palmed the silver wolf head. "Howl at the moon often, my brother." He handed over the alpha's brooch. "Stay true to our oath."

Teg refused it. "No."

"Ye must. Adaira needs our pack to defeat the queen. Ye'll need to be there for her."

"Coward." Teg threw the brooch on the bed next to Rafe. "Once a wolf, always a wolf."

"Teg..."

"Nay, I will not watch my brother surrender." Teg pulled the furs off Rafe. "I'll be outside preparing to defeat ye with my sword. Ye will fight again, wolf or not. Ye are the Mad Dog." Teg turned and quit the bedchamber.

Somewhere between the words coward and Mad Dog, something lit a fire inside Rafe. Something he hadn't felt in a long time.

With determination, Rafe swung his legs across the bed and sat on the edge of the mattress. He took the brooch and pinned it to his tunic. Aye, he was a wolf and it was time he started acting like one again. He reached for the walking stick, then stood on shaky legs. Being abed this long had weakened his body. His muscles strained to keep his big frame upright. There was no way he'd allow Teg to best him, though. The Mad Dog had been stirred to life once more.

Rafe made it to the courtyard without falling on his arse. Mayhap the staff wasn't so bad after all.

"Ye're here," Teg said as he walked toward him with sword in hand.

"I had no choice. I could not allow my wee brother to best me," Rafe teased.

"That's the spirit."

Teg tossed Rafe the sword. Rafe caught it. They shared a brief smile, then quickly stood in battle stance. Teg charged first, lifting his sword above his head, then bringing it down like a hammer.

Rafe didn't have time to think, only react. He easily blocked his brother's blow.

"I knew ye still had it in ye," Teg said through gritted teeth.

Rafe shoved him off, staggering a bit. "I might have been kicked in the ballocks, but now I'm ready to fight." One handed, Rafe swung his claymore in front of him. He lunged forward, barely missing Teg's gut. "Aye, this feels good."

With every strike, Rafe grew more and more confident. Something powerful, unlike anything he'd felt before, surged through him, racing through his veins like fire. He was quicker and stronger. He had all his wolf senses, yet he was human.

Rafe watched his brother as he circled Rafe like prey. Rafe tossed his sword to the ground, then gripped his staff in both hands. He grinned wickedly at Teg before he spun around on one leg with lightning speed. The staff connected with the back of Teg's legs, sweeping them from underneath him. He hit the ground hard.

"God's bones," Teg exclaimed. "Where did ye learn how to do that?"

Rafe was as surprised as Teg. "I don't know. I didn't think about what I was doing. I simply reacted."

"Ye didn't lose balance once," Teg said with satisfaction. "Are ye sure yer wolf is gone?"

"I cannot feel him," Rafe said, confused about his newfound strength. "There's something else inside me. 'Tis different, stronger."

They both looked at each other, stunned.

"Where's Adaira?" Rafe asked.

"I saw her on the other side of the bailey with a group of children."

Without delay, Rafe hobbled his way to the bailey as fast as he could.

He found Adaira playing with three wee girls. They were dancing around in a circle, singing. Her beauty was breathtaking and her smile shined like a ray of sunlight. He listened to their song.

"Have ye seen the wolf with big, sharp teeth? Oh, where could he be?" they sang.

The girls called out, "Could he be in the kitchen eating our food?"

Adaira smiled. "Now that he's full, oh, where could he be?"

"He's sleeping in me bed," one of the girls answered.

Rafe chuckled. If they wanted to find the wolf, they didn't have to look very far. Rafe approached the girls. As soon as Adaira saw him, she stopped and then started to sing again.

"Have ye seen the wolf with the big, sharp teeth?" They circled around, and Adaira smiled. "Oh, where could he be?"

Rafe lunged and growled. "Here I am."

The girls screamed. Two of them ran behind Adaira, hugging her. The third girl studied Rafe, unafraid. Her hair was long and black, her dark eyes shimmered as she smiled. She reminded him of Adaira when she was a child.

"'Tis only Master Rafe," the girl said as she ran up and hugged him, almost knocking him over.

"Aye, I chased the wolf away," he laughed.

"Girls, go to the kitchen and fetch ye some food," Adaira said.

The youngest, with blonde hair and blue eyes, looked up at Adaira and smiled. "Thank ye, me lady."

Adaira wiped a smudge of dirt from her cheek. She bent down. "Any time ye're hungry, come find me. Ye'll never go without."

The wee lass nodded, then took off with her sisters to the kitchen.

Seeing Adaira with children unleashed the primal beast within Rafe. He wanted to plant his seed deep inside her and watch as her stomach swelled with his child. Rafe took her in his arms. She let out a squeal of surprise. He cupped the back of her neck, pulling her into a kiss. "Christ, I've missed ye," he whispered against her lips.

"Rafe," she said breathlessly, "I'm happy to see ye out of bed."

"I've been an arse. I'm sorry."

"Ye're forgiven." Adaira laid her head on his chest and he wrapped his arms around her. "I can no' live without ye, Wolf. I'm no' sorry for what I did. I'd do it again it meant saving yer life."

"I know." He kissed the top of her head.

"Have ye felt yer wolf?"

Silence fell between them as they held each other. He felt her hold her breath as she waited for him to answer. He should tell her about the new strength he'd felt. But since he didn't completely understand it, he decided to wait.

Mayhap, it was his wolf clawing its way back to him, or it had everything to do with Adaira's blood.

"Ye are good to those girls." He intentionally changed the subject.

"'Tis a shame. Their parents died of fever and their grandmother can barely keep them clothed and fed."

"Is there anyone else in the family that can look after them?"

"Their uncle, but he's a drunk."

"Have the girls come live in the castle. Ye'd make an excellent mentor."

"Rafe, I'm a blood drinker. Once the girls find out, they'll fear me."

"Ye cannot let them starve."

Adaira stepped out of his embrace. "Ye want them to come live with us, dinnae ye?"

Rafe shrugged his shoulders. "I wouldn't say no if ye asked me."

Adaira smiled. "Can the girls live here in the castle with us?"

"Thought ye'd never ask." Rafe smiled and kissed her. "I'm forever under yer spell. Ye are the queen of my heart."

Adaira cupped his face and stared deep into his eyes. "And ye'll forever be me wolf."

20

ADAIRA SAT at the head table in the great hall overlooking her clan. The ceremony was over and she was now laird. They were her family and trusted her to defend their home, which quite frankly made her nervous. She wasn't blind, nor deaf to clan chatter. While some clansmen welcomed the new change of leadership, others weren't quick to accept the new laird. Convincing the warriors who were loyal to Cormag to fight her battles would indeed be a trying task. Without her sisters by her side, she wasn't sure if she was up for the challenge.

As she looked onward, Clan Keith was in full celebration. The tables were filled with tasty food and wine. Music played softly in the background. Mayhap her concern was misplaced.

Taking in a calming breath, she looked at Rafe. His smile instantly melted away her fears. None of this would have happened without her wolf. With him by her side, there was nothing she couldn't accomplish.

Rafe took her hands in his. "What's wrong."

"Nothing."

Rafe raised a brow. "I don't believe ye."

Adaira sighed. "I haven't heard back from Masie. I can no' shake the feeling that she has deserted me. I didnae blame her. I left her."

Rafe kissed her hands. "Have faith. Masie will be here."

"I pray it true. We need Clan Gunn's alliance if we are to defeat the queen."

"They will come."

Adaira smiled. "Ye give me faith."

Rafe leaned in and kissed her cheek.

A servant who Adaira didn't recognize filled her cup with wine. She reached for the tankard, but Rafe stopped her.

"Don't drink it."

"What?"

Rafe studied the vessel. "She didn't offer me any wine."

Adaira froze as she caught a sweet whiff of poison in the air.

Rafe grabbed the tankard and sniffed the wine. "Poison."

"Poison?" Adaira gasped.

"Someone wants ye dead." Rafe quickly stood and began to go after the lass.

Adaira grabbed his arm. "Wait. I'm going with ye."

"No. 'Tis safer if ye stay here."

"Rafe—"

"Stop arguing with me. She's getting away." Rafe strode out of the hall, following the lass's scent.

Adaira slowly sat down. How could she be so stupid? With the fae queen wanting her dead, she should have taken in-depth measures to secure her safety. Adaira chuckled in disbelief. Mayhap this was the queen's twisted way to send her a message. "Maiden, Mother, Crone." Fear struck her to the marrow with thoughts of Queen

Galanthus. What if the queen had found her? What if this was all a trick? What if this was the queen's way of luring Rafe away to capture him?

Adaira bolted from her chair; she had to find Rafe. As she left her chair, her knee slammed into something hard, knocking it over. "Och!" she reached down and rubbed her knee, then noticed Rafe's staff. Why didn't he have his staff? He couldn't walk without it.

Adaira grabbed the walking stick and strode after him, shouldering her way through the great hall. She was close to the door when Teg stopped her. "My laird, something is wrong, aye? Where's Rafe?"

"Aye, something is verra wrong. Someone tried to poison me and yer brother ran after her. He left this behind." Adaira showed him the staff.

"Shite," Teg exclaimed. "I'm going with ye."

"Fine, we must move fast."

As soon as they were outside, Teg shifted into his wolf and immediately tracked Rafe. Teg was on the hunt, running fast through the village. Adaira had no problem keeping up with him, in fact she wished he would move faster. If the queen had laid one icy finger on Rafe, she'd kill her. Adaira sucked in a breath. She wouldn't breathe easily again until they found her wolf.

They came to an abrupt stop before they reached the forest. A silver and black wolf slinked from the tree line. Adaira locked eyes on the beast and gasped. "Rafe!" Thank the gods, he was safe.

With Godspeed, she took off toward the wolf. As she got closer she noticed something wasn't right. Not only was Rafe's wolf back, he was twice the size and twice as menacing. "Oh god," she exclaimed. Was this the Mad Dog?

Not knowing if her wolf was Rafe or the Mad Dog she

abruptly halted, creating distance between them. Suddenly, Teg leapt in front of her with his fur raised, growling low and deep at his brother as to warn him to stay away.

Rafe snarled and snapped back.

A chill swept over her; different form the frigid forest weather. A dark coldness froze her where she stood as the wolves' guttural growls shook her to the core. Their lips were raised, foam flung from Rafe's mouth as he snapped his teeth at Teg. Never would Adaira have thought she'd be stuck in the middle of a standoff between two powerful wolves.

The tension between the brothers was about to break. If she didn't do something to end this, one of the wolves blood would be on her hands—and by look of Rafe's blade-sharp teeth, it would be his. Swallowing past the fear, she took a step out from behind Teg. Deep in her heart she knew Rafe would never hurt her so she began to walk closer to him. Teg snarled, disapproving. She turned around and glared. "Teg, this is yer brother. Stop it."

Teg howled as if he was calling the pack. He wasn't backing down.

"Please, Teg. Let me handle this," Adaira begged. "I know Rafe. He will no' hurt us." She turned back around and continued to approach her wolf.

As she came closer, the wolf became more fascinating. It wasn't the size of the massive beast that caused her blood to chill. Nay, there was something different laying behind his sliver depths—a darkness she knew all too well. "What have I done?"

Rafe flattened his ears as she stood in front of him. "Why didn't ye tell me that me blood has changed ye?" She tossed the staff next to him.

Rafe whimpered as he looked away from her.

"Rafe, dinnae hide behind the beast. Shift, we need to talk." Adaira placed her hands on her hips. Damn him for keeping a secret.

The wolf shook its head. Apparently Rafe didn't want to talk.

"How long have ye known?" Spellbound by the beast's beauty, her anger softened as she ran her hand down the side of his neck, admiring the softness of his fur. Rafe's wolf had always been masculine, but this creature standing in front of her was exuding vigor. She cupped his face, bringing his eyes to hers. "Ye are an amazing beast."

Rafe nudged her cheek with his nose. She closed her eyes as a tear rolled down her face. "I'm so sorry, Wolf." She held her head in her hands and fell to her knees. Not in her wildest dreams had she thought her blood would do this to him. Aye, she knew when she saved Rafe that her blood might kill his wolf. However, she didn't realize it would have the opposite effect.

His strong hands held hers and pulled her to her feet. She opened her eyes, and Rafe was now in human form. "I wanted to tell ye, but I wasn't sure what was happening to my wolf."

"Rafe, I had no idea me blood would do this to ye."

"Adaira Keith, there's nothing to be sorry for. Ye have given me strength beyond compare. 'Tis like a surge of power is pulsing through me. My senses are keener. My wolf can see in vibrant color and I can feel the earth pulling me toward something. Something even more powerful."

"It's a curse." Adaira looked away.

"What do ye mean, a curse?"

Adaira took a deep breath. She had to warn him even if the ramifications of her actions would mean losing him. "What ye're feeling is blood lust. Ye must be careful."

"I can handle it. I don't understand yer reaction to this, Adaira. Take comfort that I can now protect ye and the clan better than before."

"Nay, I dinnae take comfort in knowing what I've created." Adaira stepped out of his embrace. "Everyone has a dark side. The curse intensifies the darkness. I have turned that darkness into evil."

"My heart's queen, ye're wrong." He pulled her close. "Ye have given me a gift, and I fully intend to use it with great care. I would have never been able to track a fae without these new strengths."

"What do ye mean?"

"That lass who tried to poison ye was fae. I tracked her to a fairy mound where she disappeared."

Shocked, Adaira looked up at him. "Ye found the fairy mound?"

"Aye. 'Tis far south from here."

"Ye found the queen." Adaira's heart plummeted to her stomach. She had been right. The Unseelie fae queen knew Adaira's weakness was Rafe, and she would use him to get to her. "Ye must never go inside. Please promise me. The queen will take ye away from me."

"I promise." He kissed the top of her head. "Ye have nothing to worry about. We'll find Leana and bring her home. Ye have my word."

She wanted to believe him. However, she'd spent ten long years with the queen and seen the evil the fae was capable of. She wouldn't rest until her sisters were home and safe, and the queen was dead. She looked up at Rafe. "I have no doubt ye'll protect me. And knowing yer wolf is back and stronger than ever, gives me hope."

Rafe gripped her waist, pulling her close. He claimed

her lips, kissing her with a passion that made Adaira grow weak in the knees.

The sound of someone clearing their throat broke the kiss. Adaira looked behind her as Teg stood with his arms crossed over his chest. "Brother, for a moment there I thought I was a dead wolf."

Adaira and Rafe bellowed with laughter as Rafe put his arm around Teg.

"I've seen and heard some crazy things," Teg said. "However, this tops them all." Teg laughed as the three of them made their way back to the castle.

EPILOGUE

A DAY HAD PASSED since the gathering, and Adaira wasted no time getting right to work. Determined to succeed, she'd chosen her trusted advisors wisely to help her rule Clan Keith and East Dornoch. Seated at a table in the great room, Adaira looked out into the hall. Both wolf and man sat at opposite sides of the table. This was the first time since the battle they had met—tension was thick in the air.

Tegwyn and William sat to her right, holding back their snarls. To Adaira's left, three humans, one of them Chattan, who had served under her father and Cormag. He was a seasoned warrior with a sharp mind. She knew if she could gain his loyalty, the others would follow. It was a challenge, for old clan wounds had never completely healed.

She looked further down the table to three empty chairs. It had been over a week since she'd requested Masie's presence. She needed Clan Gunn in this fight against the fae. Since Masie was married to Laird Gunn's brother, it seemed likely that their clans would unite, but with years of feuding, there was still bad blood between them. She prayed Masie could change that.

Adaira whispered to Rafe, "She should have been here by now. I can no' stall much longer."

Rafe placed his hand on hers. "She'll be here."

Adaira nodded. It amazed her how he always knew the right words to say. He gave her the peace and strength she needed, for what she was about to do would either unite the clan or destroy their chances of defeating the queen.

"'Tis time." Adaira glanced at Rafe.

"Ye must be wondering why I called a meeting. In the past, honor has been forgotten. Our word has been tarnished by a man who hungered for power instead of fighting for his people. I want all of ye to know I will no' lead in such a way."

Adaira looked around the room. One warrior was completely ignoring her and sharpening his dirk. Another chuckled at her every word. These men weren't taking her seriously. It infuriated her and the wolves.

Adaira spoke again. "I have a plan."

"Aye, plan our next meal," one of the men called.

Rafe stood and leaned across the table, glaring at him. "Heed my words." He slammed his staff on the table. "Ye interrupt the laird one more time, I'll shove my staff so far up yer arse ye'll be spitting splinters for weeks."

The man fell silent.

Adaira continued. "There's an evil out there unlike anything ye have ever seen. I know, because I've lived with it for ten years. She's more powerful than any king. I need yer swords, yer shields, and yer unwavering will to battle for our lands and people."

"What is this threat?" Chattan asked.

At that time, the doors to the hall swung open. "She's evil. An Unseelie fae who will stop at nothing to get what she wants." Masie, Kerr, and Bhaltair entered the hall. "Sorry we're late, Adaira," Masie said with a wide grin.

"Masie!" Adaira cried out and ran to her. She hugged her sister tight. "Ye came."

"Do ye think I'd let ye kill the queen without me?"

Adaira welcomed Kerr and Bhaltair. "I'm so happy ye decided to join us."

Bhaltair bowed and kissed Adaira's hand. "We meet again."

Adaira smiled. Hope filled her heart. Finally, she might have a chance of killing the queen and regaining their freedom once and for all.

"Are ye proposing for us to ally with the Gunns and kill an evil fairy? Are ye daft?" Chattan asked.

The Keith advisors laughed.

Adaira stood next to Chattan. "Humans are no' the only living creatures. There are things out there made up of pure evil. Things ye'll never understand. If we allow the queen to go unchecked, she'll only grow more powerful." Adaira walked back to the head of the table. "Ten years ago, the queen tricked me sisters and me. She stole our freedom. She ripped us away from our family. She opened the veil unleashing her princes and wrath upon our land. She's the reason Beathen is dead. Cormag would not listen and accused me of cursing our clan. I didnae want the role of clan chieftain, but I will no' stand by and allow the queen to take this land from us."

Chattan's expression softened. "We always wondered what happened to ye girls. And yer poor mum...God rest her soul."

Adaira paused. It saddened her to have missed so much precious time with her mother. Adaira pushed those thoughts behind her. "This is an opportunity to unite Clan Keith, Clan Gunn, and the Honor Guard. I'll need every one of ye."

The room fell eerily silent. Adaira searched the men's faces, waiting for them to respond. Their cold, hardened expressions were impossible to read. With Rafe's help, she knew she had the Honor Guard by her side. But what about the others? Would they trust her?

Bhaltair stood. "Our families have feuded for hundreds of years. 'Tis time we unite. My lady, ye have our swords."

Rafe stood and turned to Adaira. "My lady, ye have our power and loyalty." He winked at her.

Chattan also stood. "Ye're Doughall's daughter." He knelt on one knee. "Ye have our trust. We'll send the beast back to hell."

"Rise, my lord. Ye shall no' bow to anyone." Tears welled in her eyes. She couldn't believe it. She now had her army and they were ready to fight. "Men, I can no' thank ye enough. I will no' let ye down." Adaira nodded, dismissing the men.

Masie ran up to Adaira and hugged her. "I can no' believe it. Me sister, Laird of Clan Keith."

"Och, Masie, I thought ye were mad at me for leaving ye at Ravens Landing. I was scared ye wouldn't come back."

"No matter what, ye are me sister. I'll always be loyal to ye." Masie looked around the room. "Where's Leana?"

"Masie, I dinnae know where she is."

"What do ye mean? I thought ye left Ravens Landing together."

"We did. But we got separated."

"Nay, Sister, she wanted to leave us."

Adaira's brows creased in confusion. "But why would she want to leave us?"

"'Tis the same reason ye left me at Ravens Landing," Masie said.

Realization washed over Adaira. She knew exactly why Leana had left. "She thinks she's protecting us."

"Aye."

"Masie, I'm afraid. She can no' take on the queen by herself."

"I know. But she feels responsible for the mess we're in. We need to find her."

"I will go and search for yer sister," Tegwyn said. "I know where to start."

"And I will go as well," Bhaltair offered. "I promised Masie I'd find Leana. I owe her for saving my life."

Adaira looked at Masie, then to Rafe. "Teg is the best tracker in our pack. He should go," Rafe said. "I can spare fifty men, for we need the rest here to prepare for the queen."

"Nay." Bhaltair walked over to Adaira. "Too many men will scare her. Just the two of us. That's it."

"I don't need any help," Teg said.

"I think Bhaltair is right," Adaira said. "Teg, ye'll go with him and find my sister. Kerr and Rafe, I'll need ye here to prepare our men for battle."

"Aye," Kerr agreed.

"Now that everything is settled," William said, "A celebration for the new chieftain awaits us. "Let the ale flow and the women be bonny."

Adaira laughed as the great hall emptied.

Rafe took her in his arms. "My queen, ye were born to lead."

"Does it bother ye?" Adaira touched the neckline of his tunic.

"Not at all. I already have everything I want right here in my arms."

"I love ye, Wolf."

"And I, ye."

BOOK 3 WICKED DARKNESS - SNEAK PEEK

CHAPTER I

Evil lingered in the air. And for someone like Leana, who had fallen from grace so long ago, it felt perfect. Masked by her black cloak, she slipped inside the familiar tavern she'd been visiting for over a month, chose her usual seat in the back of the room, and wondered where a certain woman had gotten to. Leana's latest target, a lass that never deviated from her daily routine.

"Wine?" A voice asked a nearby patron.

Leana closed her eyes and breathed in the intoxicating fragrance of heather and bog myrtle. The killer inside her resurfaced, dominating her every thought. Her gums ached as she recalled how easily her fangs could rip into flesh. Especially the soft skin on a delicate neck. *Ye must be patient, Leana,* her darker side warned. She found it difficult to resist her natural cravings, that constant temptation to revert back to her lower self, the creature that preyed upon the weak.

Leana wasn't ashamed of who or what she was—she wore it proud like a crown upon her head. She gripped the edge of the table, her sharp black nails splintering the wood. She hadn't spent the last month studying Davina's every move just to surrender to her hunger and ruin everything she'd planned so carefully. If she'd intended for the lass to be a simple meal, she would have killed her the first day. Nay, this time Leana had a purpose.

She'd watched Davina and knew her every move as if it were her own. With her eyes closed, Leana heard the wine splashing into the tankard at the next table, even smelled her hair. Her flirtatious laughter made Leana smile. *Aye, the lass was perfect.*

Leana opened her eyes to find Davina standing next to her. The lass didn't look well. Her eyes were swollen and red and her skin much paler than the day before.

"Mistress." Davina coughed into a cloth. The stench of blood awakened the *Baobhan sith's* hunger inside Leana.

"Please, sit," Leana motioned to the chair across the table. "Ye need rest."

"I can no'." The lass looked around the tavern. "I must get back to work."

Leana pulled back her hood and stared into the lass's eyes. "Ye want to sit with me, Davina." With a single look, Leana could influence the mind of a human, bend Davina to her will.

Confusion creased Davina's face. "How do ye know my name?"

"There's no one here but ye and I."

Davina sat down.

Luck was on Leana's side. The stronger willed the victim, the harder it was to manipulate their mind. But Davina was different—she was ill. Her mind was weak. "Ye are no' well, lass."

"How do ye know?"

"I can smell heather and bog myrtle on yer breath. Everyone knows that's a remedy for fever. I know what ails ye."

"How? Can ye see the demon?"

Demon? That was ridiculous. It was clear the lass was suffering from a weak heart.

"The priest said I should ask God for forgiveness for my sins. God is punishing me, but for what, I dinnae know."

Leana held the lass's hand. "There's no' demon in ye. Ye have a failing heart."

Leana sat back, watching Davina. Compassion broke through her savagery, planting the tiniest seed of sympathy for the lass. She could heal Davina. *"Keep yer promise to yer sisters. Dinnae take an innocent life,"* her conscious warned.

But Davina had something Leana wanted—her life.

The unfortunate lass matched Leana in every way with her long red hair, slender body, and pale skin. She had no family, so no one would notice if she disappeared and Leana took over her body.

Faking her own death was the only way for Leana to trick the fae queen into believing she had died. The queen wanted her, for it was Leana who had called upon the fae for help. She'd made the blood oath that had changed her sisters' lives.

With Leana gone, her sisters, Adaira and Masie, would stop searching for her and live productive lives. It was the only way to protect them. In the past Leana had always tried to do the right thing, but always ended up hurting someone she loved. Not this time.

Leana exhaled. This wasn't the time for her conscious to take a righteous stance.

"Lass." Leana leaned forward. "I can take yer pain away. All ye have to do is ask." If Davina wanted to end her suffering, it wouldn't feel like Leana had taken an innocent life. The fae queen had taught her so well.

"I dinnae understand," Davina said. "The priest said I would die. How can ye heal me?"

"Lass, I never said I would heal ye. All I said was I can take the pain away. No more coughing up blood, no more weakness, no more pain." Leana looked around the tavern. "Ye would no' have to work here anymore. Dinnae ye grow tired of men putting their hands all over ye?"

"Aye." Davina coughed.

"Dinnae ye want to leave all this loneliness behind?"

"Aye."

"I can give ye what ye seek."

"Death?"

"All ye have to do is ask."

Davina lowered her head. "I'm in so much pain."

"I know, lass." Leana squeezed her hand. Sorrow welled in Davina's eyes causing Leana's cold heart to crack with sympathy.

"I've wasted my life. I was too scared to live outside these four walls." Davina looked around the Tavern. "My dreams of marrying a loving man never came true. I should have conquered life and taken what I wanted. Instead, I stayed here with the bottom of the barrel eejits." Davina sobbed into her hands.

Leana caught a tear from Davina's cheek. The loneliness, regret, and agony that plagued the lass filled Leana with immeasurable hunger. If she wasn't careful, her inner beast would be unleashed. "Ask me," Leana commanded.

Davina slowly looked up from the floor. She stared into Leana's eyes, completely bewitched.

"Good, lass," Leana whispered. "Ye want to ask me something, aye?"

Davina nodded. "Take me to the void. Kill me."

Leana's lips curled into a wicked grin. The plan was working beautifully. Manipulating Davina's mind was too easy. "Ye will obey every word I say."

Davina nodded.

"Ye can no' breathe."

The lass clutched her chest and gasped for air.

"Ye need fresh air. Go outside and wait for me."

"Aye." Davina quickly stood.

"Dinnae talk to anyone. Go unseen," Leana said.

The lass made her way out of the tavern.

Relieved, Leana exhaled. No matter how many times she'd controlled a human's mind, it still made her nervous. The mind was powerful and unpredictable. If one thing went wrong, an unexpected scream or a bold accusation against her, Leana could be accused of witchery and burned at the stake. Nay, she wasn't going to become kindling for a bonfire.

Leana pulled her hood over her head and walked outside. Her new life awaited.

The cold, night air bit into Leana's skin as she followed Davina's footprints into the glen behind the tavern. Her blood pumped wildly through her veins with the need to kill. Aye, Davina waited just beyond the trees. Leana licked her lips as everything turned red. Her fangs extended, and animal-like power consumed her. Shite, the beast was there. Like lightening, she stalked through the glen—ready to attack, ready to kill, ready to change her own life.

She found her prey standing beside the shallow grave she'd dug earlier.

"How long have ye been planning me death?" Davina asked.

The lass's mind was under Leana's control, so why was she asking questions? Had she missed something about Davina? "Who are ye?"

"Ye should know. Ye've been stalking me."

What was happening? Had Leana been tricked? Was the queen behind this? Perhaps she should go before something happened…

"Dinnae leave," Davina said. "I want to die. And it's my choice. But why me? Why am I chosen?"

Leana didn't know what to say, nor was she obligated to explain herself. "The real question here is why I can no' compel yer mind." Leana studied Davina. "What are ye?"

"What do ye mean? I'm an orphan. 'Tis all I know."

"But ye know who—" Leana paused. Mayhap the lass didn't know that a blood drinker was standing in front of her.

"Know what?"

"The truth is, I want yer life and I can no' have it if ye're still alive."

"Why would ye want to be me? I'm nothing."

"Davina, yer life matters to me."

"Why? Who are ye running from?"

Maiden, Mother, Crone. "It does no' matter why I chose ye or who I'm running from." *Because ye'll be dead.* "Ye'll no longer suffer. This life was no' yers to keep. Face death and cross into the void knowing yer new life begins in another time and place."

Davina braved looking at Leana.

The first time Leana had seen Davina, her eyes were

filled with sorrow. Perhaps that's what had attracted her to Davina, for Leana knew endless suffering, too. Something altogether different shined in the lass's eyes now. A flicker of something good. *Hope?*

"Who will send me to the void?" Davina asked.

"My name is Leana."

"Leana, promise ye'll live my life better than I have."

Once again, the lass had found a way to creep into Leana's heart. She paused, considering Davina's words carefully. If she healed the lass *Davina* could live her own life to its fullest. She'd find the man of her dreams, have many bairns.

Did Leana have the strength to ward off these weak human feelings and allow this woman to live?

Me sisters deserve to live. Davina must die.

"I promise."

The lass tipped her chin up. "I am ready."

Leana brushed Davina's long hair away from her face. A large vein ran down the side of her neck, her sweet life essence running through it. Leana's gums ached as her fangs descended.

Without a second thought, Leana's fangs stabbed through Davina's tender flesh. She sucked at the vein. Iron-tasting blood flowed across her tongue and down her throat, awaking her eternal thirst.

It didn't take long for Davina to wilt against Leana, too weak to stand on her own. Leana took another long taste, sealing Davina's fate. Her body went limp and her heart stopped beating.

Leana laid the body on the ground. She wiped the blood from her mouth with the back of her hand, catching her breath. She felt empty and numb. Though her plan had worked, she didn't feel any better. Why did she feel like there was something gripping at her heart and wouldn't let go? Remorse? Nay, she shook her head and quickly dismissed that wretched thought. She'd killed before, but somehow, this felt different.

Quickly, Leana switched dresses with the lass, then placed Davina in the grave. Looking down at Davina, Leana shuddered. By switching clothes with the lass, Davina took on Leana's features. She picked up the shovel she'd left by the grave earlier and started to fill the grave with dirt. That's when she found her green, woolen cloak on the ground. She picked it up. Her Clan Keith white stag brooch was pinned to the cloak, and it reminded Leana of her sisters. Their mother had given them matching brooches. It was the only thing she had left from her family. She caressed the heirloom.

Everything must die with the lass.

Keeping anything that tied her to Leana Keith was a risk she wasn't willing to take. She threw the cloak and brooch inside the half-filled grave, then resumed shoveling. "The demons can no' harm ye anymore, Davina. Yer God will lay ye to rest." At least she hoped so for the lass's sake. "Goodbye, Leana Keith."

About Victoria Zak

Victoria Zak is an internationally bestselling author of historical and contemporary romance. She weaves magic into her timeless tales, reminding readers anything is possible, especially with a dragon by your side. Raised in Dunedin, Florida, the sister city to Stirling, Scotland, no wonder she grew up fascinated with anything Scottish. Add the ocean into the mix, and it's easy to see where Victoria found inspiration for her stories.

As a child, she read anything she could get her hands on, which developed into full-scale book addiction by adulthood. Curious by nature, Victoria doesn't shy away from anything. She enjoys historical research and people watching is her favorite sport. Victoria currently resides in Maryland with her real-life heroes, her husband and two children.

Victoria loves to hear from her readers. You can connect with her through the links below:

www.victoriazakromance.com
victoria@victoriazakromance.com

MORE BOOKS BY VICTORIA ZAK

Guardians of Scotland Series:

Highland Burn

Highland Storm

Highland Fate

Highland Destiny

Daughters of Highland Darkness Series:

Beautiful Darkness

Deadly Darkness

Wicked Darkness (2018)

Hell's Cowboys Series:

My Immortal Cowboy

Stand Alones:

De Wolfe's Honor

Once Upon a Winter Solstice

The Jewel of Grim Fortress

Midnight's Kiss